A FAMILY FOR THE RANCHER

ALLISON B. COLLINS

MILLS & BOON

First Published in Great Britain 2018
by Mills & Boon, an imprint of HarperCollins*Publishers*
1 London Bridge Street, London, SE1 9GF

A Family for the Rancher © 2018 Allison B. Collins

ISBN: 978-0-263-26475-3

38-0218

MIX
Paper from
responsible sources
FSC™ C007454

This book is produced from independently certified FSC™ paper to ensure responsible forest management.

For more information visit: www.harpercollins.co.uk/green

Printed and bound in Spain
by CPI, Barcelona

This book is dedicated to the best friends and
critique partners any author could ask for:
Sasha Summers, Suzanne Clark and Angela Hicks.
Thanks for being on this wild ride with me!

To Johanna Raisanen,
thank you for loving my manuscript
and bringing me into the family.

And to my aunt Pat, whose comments about
a cowboy on the back roads of Colorado
inspired the character of Bunny Randolph.

But most of all to my husband, Joe.
Hero, best friend, excellent vacation planner
and the love of my life.
You're the best, Mister!

Chapter One

Nash Sullivan leaned his head on Thunder's solid shoulder, the muscles flexing beneath his cheek. The scent of hay, sun and saddle soap brought back a tidal wave of memories. Their first rodeo together, long days of riding the fences, riding bareback out to his sanctuary at the pond. He ached to get back in the saddle again after his long stint in the Army riding in nothing but military trucks and tanks the last ten years.

Now he couldn't even climb into the saddle. He stepped away, but Thunder shifted, nudged Nash back against his shoulder.

His gut clenched, and while he wouldn't, couldn't, admit it to anyone, he loved this damn horse, and for the first time, it felt right being home again.

"Need a mounting block, son?"

The words stung, but he couldn't let his dad know. Thunder shifted and snorted, stomping the hard-packed Montana dirt in front of him.

He pulled the reins tighter and whispered to the brown gelding. Once Thunder had quieted, he lifted his left leg and guided his foot into the stirrup. Thunder shifted, and Nash tightened his thigh muscles, or what was left of them, to get up. Instead he had to haul his foot out as the horse snorted again and stepped away.

"I told you it was too soon. You've only been out of the hospital a few months." His dad walked up to Thunder and patted his neck. "I want you to take charge of the horses."

"Now? Why?" He squinted in the sunlight, noticing just how gray his dad's hair had gotten over the years. Even his beard was gray. But the old man was still fit, with ramrod straight posture and a swagger that showed one and all he owned their guest ranch and was proud of it.

"Curly's making retirement noises again, and this time I think he's serious. You still want the job, right?"

"You know I do."

"Just checking. Last time you said you wanted it, you left for ten years."

"I was doing my duty."

"And I'm proud of you for it. But you were seriously injured and aren't back to normal yet."

Nash held very still, anger and fear forming a cannonball in his gut.

"Curly and his wife want to move to Arizona by autumn, and I want you ready to step in as soon as he leaves. I've hired a physical therapist to come out here and get you in shape."

"I don't need a therapist. I'll be fine," he said over his shoulder, and handed the reins to a ranch hand. Limping, every step agony, he headed to his truck, yanked the door open and clumsily climbed in. Shoving the key in the ignition, he cranked the engine and stomped on the gas pedal, leaving a spray of dirt and grass in his wake.

Angus Sullivan hadn't been such an SOB when their mother had been alive. *Dammit. Why'd he go and hire a therapist?* Images of the last old biddy he'd had to go through physical therapy with at the hospital in Germany popped into his mind. She was another drill sergeant, humorless, cantankerous, dry—same age as his dad.

Slamming to a halt in front of his cabin, he climbed out of the truck and hobbled inside. He locked the door and yanked the curtains closed, covering the wall of glass that overlooked the sparkling blue lake.

The bar on the other side of the big open living room yielded a bottle of whiskey—glass not needed. He'd picked this cabin to settle into because of the bar, and he'd made sure it was fully stocked his second day home.

Turning to head toward the couch, a knife-sharp pain stabbed through his thigh. Gritting his teeth, he stopped and breathed through the throbbing like the old bat had taught him. Once it was under control, he grabbed an ice pack out of the freezer and sat down, hoisting his leg onto the beat-up trunk he used as a coffee table.

He set the ice pack over his thigh, then drank deeply from the whiskey bottle, relishing the heat as it went down.

Tipping the bottle again, his eye caught the sports trophies and silver buckles gleaming on the shelves, mocking him.

Grabbing the remote, he turned the TV on. Bombs exploded as the screen lit up, and he flinched, hitting the mute button as fast as he could. He jabbed at the channel button, but it seemed as if every other station was showing either an old war movie or a sappy chick flick.

"Where the hell are the baseball games?"

A knock sounded at the door. He gulped another swallow of whiskey, decided to ignore it. Probably one of his brothers come to tell him to apologize to their dad. *Well, screw that. I ain't in the mood.*

Another knock and he swigged more whiskey.

This time someone pounded on the door. He stood and

had to catch his balance on the arm of the couch, then limped to the front door, every step burning his thigh. He yanked the door open, saw his youngest brother standing on the stoop.

"What the hell do you want, Hunter? I'm not apologizing to him. Now leave me alone." He started to slam the door when Hunter moved aside, revealing a petite woman standing on the porch.

Her black hair was braided, the tail curving over her shoulder and down almost to her waist, but a few strands had escaped and blew in the breeze, teasing her sculpted cheekbones. Startling blue eyes stared at him long enough to make him almost ashamed of his snarls.

"Ma'am," he said, the manners his momma ingrained in him bursting forth.

"This is Kelsey Summers," Hunter said, putting a hand on her back to guide her past him, shoving Nash back a few steps. "She's your therapist."

His temper peaked again, hitting the boiling point. "I told him I don't need a therapist. You can go now." Tilting the bottle again, he drained the last of it. He wavered, tempted to leave them there so he could grab a full bottle, or shove them out first. Another pain slashed through his leg, and the question was settled—whiskey first.

But he turned too quickly, and his leg couldn't keep up. He went down hard on his good knee, and his thigh went from simmering to burning hot.

Hunter rushed over and grabbed his arm, but Nash shoved him away, cursing a blue streak.

Hunter backed away, hands held up. "Hey, bro. Just trying to help."

"I don't need your help, or Dad's help, or this woman's help." He blew out a breath and braced his arm on the side table to stand up. Wincing, he gently put weight on his bad leg.

"Why don't I be the judge of that? Come on and sit down." Kelsey gestured toward the couch.

Her voice was quiet, just a little throaty, and held a twang of the South in it.

"No thanks. I'm fine."

She crossed her arms in front of her and cocked a hip. "Sure you are. Feels like fire racing through your quads, right? Have to be careful when you put weight on it?"

He looked away, hating that she was right.

"Let me just look at it, then you can kick me out if you really think you don't need me."

He glanced at his brother, wanting to knock the smirk off his face. "Get out. Little lady here wants to check me out. Might get a bit personal here." He grinned, but without any humor. Maybe if he made her uncomfortable enough she'd leave on her own. Sliding his arm around her shoulders, he started to lead her to the bedroom.

Kelsey raised her hand up to his and grabbed his thumb, pulling it down, then stepped around to wrench his arm behind his back.

His arm hurt like hell, and he made sure not to move and antagonize her any further.

Hunter burst out laughing. "Well I guess I don't have to worry about Kelsey out here by herself." He opened the door and slapped his Stetson on his head. "Call me if you need a rescue, bro." He slammed the door behind him, and his laughter echoed on the breeze outside.

She let go of Nash's thumb, then stepped away from him.

He rubbed the offended thumb and stared at her. "Sorry. Just want to be alone."

Picking up the empty whiskey bottle, she said, "Why?

So you can drown your sorrows in this stuff?" She plunked it down on the table. "I'm just here to help you, okay?"

Memories assaulted him of the friends who couldn't get back to their wives and kids—their lives—because of that last mission.

"Why don't you take your jeans off and I'll assess your leg, okay? Do you want to do it in here, or in the bedroom?"

Her throaty voice saying *bedroom* made him twitch, the first sign of life down there in a long time. Bedroom probably wasn't a good idea, nor was taking off any article of clothing.

He raised an eyebrow at her.

Red crept into her creamy cheeks, but she stood up straight and picked up her medical bag. "Get a move on, Mr. Sullivan. I don't have all day to stand around here while you put the moves on me."

Pretty *and* gutsy.

He clomped into the bedroom and slammed the door. Grabbing an old pair of gym shorts from the dresser, he stripped out of his jeans. He hauled himself back out to the living room and almost fell onto the couch as a wave of exhaustion hit him.

"Um…"

Dreading to look up and see the pity, he finally raised his eyes to see Kelsey staring at his leg.

"Your dad didn't tell me you have a prosthetic leg."

"Souvenir of the Taliban."

"Why didn't he tell me?"

"Doesn't know."

The silence drew out so long he finally glanced up at her again.

"He doesn't know?"

"And don't you tell him, or any of my brothers—got it?"

"How many brothers?"

"Four."

"And no one knows."

"Yep. Can we get this over with? Got things to do."

"Like drinking more whiskey and watching TV?"

He frowned. "None of your business."

Kelsey sat down on the old trunk and unwrapped the bandage from his left leg. "Oh my God. How long has your thigh been this red?"

He looked down and saw slashes of red interspersed with the white scars. "I don't know. It's been hurting more the last few days."

"Don't you unwrap it at night and take off your prosthesis?"

Shutting his eyes, he blocked out the image of her removing the hated brace, leaving just the stump of his leg. "No," he said, his voice strangled in his throat.

"Mr. Sullivan, you need to take better care of yourself. That means taking your prosthesis off and giving your body a rest."

A cool hand smoothed over his thigh, and he jerked. He stared down at her small hand as she touched the sore spots gently. "I don't think you have any infection," she murmured, her hand going a little too close for comfort. "But the fit may be a bit off on this."

He grabbed a throw pillow from behind him and set it on his groin, folding his hands over it. Glancing at her, he thought he caught a slight smile as she turned her head away, examining the top of the prosthesis.

The persistent ache started to ease off. Maybe he should listen to the docs and follow their regimen. A stab of guilt made him jerk. His men were beyond pain, so this was all he deserved.

She set the leg down on the floor, out of sight. Pulling a bottle of lotion out of her bag, she poured some in her hand and rubbed them together. "This may be a little cool, but it should help ease the aches." Beginning right above where his knee should have been, she started rubbing slowly.

"I'm not gonna smell girlie, am I?" he asked, embarrassed at having her examine the ugliness he hated day in and day out.

She smiled, and he noticed a freckle above the corner of her lip. He stared at it, fascinated for some reason.

"No, this is the non-girlie type of lotion."

Why hadn't he noticed before how pretty she was? Her upper lip hinted at a slight overbite that was strangely arresting. Her small, graceful hands were definitely working some kind of magic.

The front door opened and Kade walked in. "Hey, here's the DVD you—"

Nash grabbed the old woven blanket off the back of the couch and threw it over his legs. "Don't you know how to knock?" he snapped.

Kade, his younger brother by a year, glanced at Kelsey as she removed her hands from beneath the blanket. His cheeks reddened, and Nash had to grin—it wasn't easy to throw Kade off his game.

"This is Kelsey. Dad hired her for me. My brother Kade."

Kade's eyebrows lifted, and he looked from one to the other, obviously still at a loss for words.

She stood up, soothing the remaining lotion into her arms. "Hi. Just to clear up whatever thoughts you have running through your dirty little mind, I'm a physical and occupational therapist. Your dad hired me to come out here and work with Nash."

Kade's cheeks were on fire, and for some reason Nash took perverse pleasure in the fact that he was embarrassed.

"NICE TO MEET you, Kelsey." Kade looked back at Nash. "Why do you still need a therapist? I thought your leg was better."

A growl erupted from the couch, startling her. She glanced at Nash, alarmed at how red his face had gotten.

"Get out. Now."

Kade took a step back. "Geez, what's wrong with you?"

She cleared her throat. "Kade, do you mind leaving? I still need to go over some things with Nash, and have to leave here shortly to pick up my daughter."

"Sure thing. Nice meeting you." Kade walked out the door, slamming it behind him.

Sitting back down on the trunk next to the couch, she pulled the blood pressure cuff and stethoscope out of her bag. "Arm, please." She glanced at his narrowed eyes. "You know, my five-year-old gets that expression on her face when I tell her it's nap time."

A look of surprise crossed his rugged face, and he finally chuckled. "Look, I'm sorry."

"We seem to have gotten off on the wrong foot today."

He glared at her, and she could have sworn steam billowed out of his ears.

"Too soon?"

"Yeah. Let's just get this over with. I need a drink." He scrubbed a hand over his face, then through his militarily short brown hair.

"Sorry." She steeled herself, strapping the cuff to his upper arm. His muscular upper arm. No doubt he'd be a difficult patient, and she'd have to call on all her patience in order to deal with this cowboy. This tall, strong, tough, knock-her-down gorgeous cowboy.

"Hey, ease up, okay?"

Crap. "As red as your face is, I figured your BP would be high." She turned the knob and air started escaping as she listened for the beats. "It's somewhat high, but that could be the alcohol."

"Doubt it. And I'd rather drink than get hooked on painkillers."

"You won't get hooked on booze?"

"Nah."

"So why did you get upset when Kade walked in?"

He looked away. "I never get any privacy now. Someone's always checking on me. I just want them to leave me alone."

"They love you, Nash. They're your family."

"They're nosy. I don't want them around all the time. I spent ten years in the Army, from regular tour of duty on base, then deployed to Afghanistan and stationed in the desert, practically living nose to ass with people."

"And they might walk in and discover your secret."

"Maybe."

"I see. May I ask why?"

"My business. And don't you say anything. They just think I was wounded, not that I lost the whole bottom half of my damned leg. In fact, I don't need you to come out anymore. Thanks for stopping by."

"So you're ready to resume your life here on the ranch. Ride horses, pitch hay, rope poor baby cows, or whatever you do on a ranch."

The glare returned to his face, his eyebrows lowering in a scowl over steely gray-blue eyes. He muttered under his breath.

"Sure you weren't in the Navy?"

"What?" he asked, confusion on his face.

"You swear like a sailor."

His mouth twitched, and a laugh rumbled out of his chest. "Okay, sorry." He blew out a breath. "Maybe I do need help, but I don't know if you're the right person for it."

"Why? I'm licensed as both phys—"

"I couldn't get on my damned horse earlier today. I need someone who can help me do that."

"Actually, I can. I grew up around horses, so in school I studied equine therapy. It'll take some time, but we can probably get you back in the saddle. Anything else you want my help with?"

"I haven't gotten la—"

"Uh-uh, mister. Your dad will have to hire someone else for *that.*"

He cracked a half grin, and darned if her heart didn't go pitter-patter. Nash Sullivan was a handful, and she'd have to stay on her toes around him. She'd had love once, and lost it. No use looking for it again.

Not when her husband's death nearly broke her.

Chapter Two

The next morning, Kelsey knocked on the heavy oak door to Nash's cabin. She waited, then knocked again. A loud crash reverberated through the door, and she pounded louder. Still no answer. She tried the handle, and to her surprise, it opened. Rushing inside, she scanned the rustic living room and kitchen.

"Mr. Sullivan? Where are you? Are you okay?"

Loud groans echoed down the hallway, and she hurried in that direction. "Mr. Sullivan?" She knocked on the bedroom door. Another loud grunt. "Nash, I'm coming in." The door opened into a cozy bedroom, and she searched for her new patient in the dim light.

Stepping farther into the room, she finally saw him lying on the floor near the dresser. She hurried over and knelt beside him. "Are you injured? Where does it hurt?"

He shoved her back. "No! I have to go back. I have to get them out."

It finally dawned on her that he must be caught up in a nightmare. Gently, she shook his shoulder. "Wake up, Nash." He still wasn't waking, and the terrified expression on his face scared her.

He flailed an arm and hit her shoulder. She caught his hand and tried to hold it still, wondering how to wake him up.

"Commander, wake up now," she all but shouted, hoping her voice would penetrate his dream.

Nash's eyes slowly opened, and he squinted at her. "Where are my men? Who are you?"

She leaned over him and switched on the lamp, bathing the room in light. "Come on, let's get you up. I'm Kelsey, remember? Your therapist."

He sat up and scooted back to lean against the dresser, scrubbed a hand over his sweaty face.

Wanting to give him a moment of privacy, she stood and headed into the bathroom. Flipping the light on, she noted a big Jacuzzi tub in the corner and a large glassed-in shower. For being a ranch in Montana, this place sure was luxurious. Dark towels hung on the rack by the shower, and she grabbed a washcloth, ran it under cold water in the sink. She wrung it out and hurried back to him.

He still sat on the floor, his good leg drawn up, arms resting on his knee, hands covering his face. The gray cotton gym shorts he'd put on yesterday were all he wore, and she couldn't help drinking in his broad shoulders, muscled chest and arms, even the scars crisscrossed on his stomach.

"Here, Mr. Sullivan, let's get you off the floor." She bent over to help him up, but he shoved her hand away.

"Leave me alone. Please," he rasped, his voice strangled.

Her heart broke for him. He had a lot more scars on the inside than out. She sank down on the floor beside him and nudged him with the cool washcloth. "Want to talk about it?"

He took the cloth from her and rubbed it over his face. "Not really."

"Were you dreaming about the war?"

He finally lowered both arms and looked at her. "What part of 'not really' did you miss?"

"I just thought it might help if you talk—get it out of your head." She stood up. "Come on, we need to get your therapy going." She reached to help him up, but he ignored her.

Moving slow, he turned on the floor and braced himself against the dresser as he rose. Wood crutches stood in the corner, and he stretched farther to grab them.

She kept still, knowing from the hard lines of determination bracketing his lips he wouldn't want her help. "I'll be out in the living room," she said, and walked out. Other patients had been stubborn about rehab and therapy. She'd just have to keep after him until she won him over.

NASH FINISHED BRUSHING his teeth and stuck the toothbrush in the holder on the counter. Without thinking, he glanced at himself in the mirror. Anger and despair bubbled to the surface once again as he caught sight of the scars. He'd practically named them—one for each of the men he'd lost.

A knock echoed through his bedroom. "Mr. Sullivan? You okay in there?"

He rolled his eyes but sucked it up and grabbed the crutches, swung out of the bathroom. He strapped on his prosthetic leg and threw on a T-shirt, loose sweats and sneakers, then hauled the door open. "Might as well call me Nash since I can't get rid of you."

She smiled. "Stubborn is a family trait, so it comes in handy sometimes. Shall we get started?"

They spent the morning working on exercises to strengthen his thighs, and by the time they were finished, he'd sweated through his T-shirt. Mopping his face off with a towel, he asked, "When can I get back on a horse?"

Kelsey stacked her equipment against the wall. "Let's shoot for a couple of weeks, okay?"

"That long? I need to be up and riding faster than that."

"Why? What's the rush?"

He turned away and paced to the refrigerator. "Strong tourist season this year, and our ranch is full this summer. I need to help." Opening a bottle of water, he drank deep.

"How long have you been home from the hospital?"

"Few months."

"And you were in for how long?"

"Five."

"You don't seem to understand that recovery from an injury like this takes time. We can't rush it, or we'll be doing more harm than good."

He handed her a bottle of water and opened another for himself. "I need to get to work. I'm out of the military, so I need to earn a living."

"Nash, please. Talk to your family. I'm sure they'll under—"

"No. Final answer." He opened the door. "I suppose you're coming back tomorrow for another torture session?"

"Yes. And I'm bringing my medieval bag of tricks for you."

Feisty. "What time shall I expect the full rack?"

"Probably a little later than today. I have to look at a rental property."

"I thought you lived in town."

She shook her head. "Just moved here with my mom and daughter, so we're in a motel until we can find a house. Place I was ready to sign on last night fell through."

Guilt pricked him. She was driving an hour each way every day to help him, and he hadn't been very nice. He brushed the guilt aside. It wasn't like *he'd* invited her into his life of hell.

"Kelsey, I was hoping I'd catch you before you left."

Nash turned at the sound of his dad's voice from the front porch. Kelsey brushed past him, her fresh scent drifting on the air toward him.

"Mr. Sullivan, it's nice to see you again."

"Did I hear you're looking for a place to live?"

"Yes, sir. I am."

"I have just the thing for you, if you're interested. There's a cabin less than a quarter mile from here. Three bedrooms, two full baths, fully equipped kitchen."

Nash's temper rose. He didn't want her here to begin with, and now she was moving in?

"Thank you, sir, but I couldn't impose on you like this. I have a young daughter, and my mother lives with us."

Relieved that she'd turned down his dad's offer, he moved to go back inside.

"No imposition at all," his dad replied.

What the hell? He tried to catch his dad's attention and stop this bad idea from going further, but the old man kept talking like he hadn't seen Nash shaking his head.

Just like always. Angus Sullivan ran roughshod, forcing his way of thinking onto his sons.

"You can live there as long as you like, or until you find a place of your own. It's just sitting empty right now. And you can put your daughter in our ranch day care. The woman who runs it is fully licensed. One of the benefits we have for our employees."

"You're so kind, Mr. Sullivan."

"No kindness at all. You're the one who has to put up with my surly son, so it's the least I can do. In fact, feel free to use any of the guests' amenities—swimming, riding, cookouts. There's a party tomorrow night—you and your family are welcome to attend. Our annual mid-summer barbecue."

"Thank you, sir."

"If you're through with Nash for the day, I'll take you over to see the cabin right now. Just follow me." His dad glanced back at him. If Nash didn't know better, he'd have sworn there was a gleam in his eye.

"See you tomorrow, Nash," she said, then got in her car.

"Dad, I don't think this is a good idea."

A loud screech, followed by a groan, then a backfire had them both wincing as Kelsey started her car.

"This will keep her from having to drive all hours of the day and night in that piece of shit car. Besides, don't you want to get better?"

Fury rose, making him grind his teeth. He limped back into the cabin and slammed the door. The rapid-fire staccato of his dad's laughter dug in deep, and he flinched.

Chapter Three

Kelsey zipped up her jeans and looked in the mirror standing in the corner of her bedroom. Butterflies fluttered in her belly, and she smoothed a hand over the pink-and-white gingham shirt. She hated parties, hated the small talk, hated how lonely she always felt at gatherings now that Rob was gone. He'd been the one to talk to everyone, made sure she was included in conversations and never left her alone. Now she avoided parties like the proverbial plague.

But she'd let it slip to her mom while they were moving into the big cabin by the lake the day before that Mr. Sullivan had invited them to the barbecue. Nothing could keep Bunny Randolph from a social gathering.

"You ready, pumpkin? We need to get going so we aren't late."

She turned around as her mom walked in the door. Bound and determined to remain youthful looking, her freshly blond hair was curled to perfection.

"Kelsey Anne, is that what you're wearing? Why don't you put on a dress?" The words were punctuated with a swirl of her mother's flowered skirt.

"Mom, it's a barbecue. It'll be outside. In the dirt."

"But men will be there, honey. Cowboys."

Her mom's eyes gleamed, and Kelsey fought not to roll her eyes.

"I'm not interested in meeting any of them. I've got my hands full already with my patient."

"Ooh! I can't wait to meet hi—"

"Mom, no. He's not a potential date, lover, boyfriend or husband. He's my patient, and when he's back up and running, we'll be moving on to the next job."

Her mother's lips pouted. "I don't see why you can't dress up just a little. Show your appreciation for all Mr. Sullivan has done for us. Thank goodness he offered you this cabin. I couldn't stand being cooped up in that motel one minute longer. I don't see why the hospital couldn't have helped out with the cost since you didn't get the job we moved here for."

"Once again, it's not the hospital's fault they lost the funding for a therapist. I just need to scrimp a little more and we can move on."

The pout hadn't left her mother's red-lacquered lips, so she linked arms with her and pulled her toward the door. "Now we need to head on down to the lodge. Just because I'm not interested in the party doesn't mean you can't have fun. Okay?"

"All right."

They walked in to the living room, and Kelsey still couldn't believe her luck that they'd be living here for the time being. It was like a log cabin on steroids, with luxurious yet comfortable furnishings and plenty of Western decor.

Floor-to-ceiling windows overlooked the clear-as-a-bell lake edged with towering trees. This morning she'd been sipping a cup of steaming tea on the patio when two elk had wandered along the lakeshore, stopping to drink as the sun peeked over the mountain, turning their coats golden.

With the pile of debts Rob had left after his death, she hadn't thought they'd ever get to stay in anything so nice. Especially for free.

Her daughter sat on the floor playing with an old plastic tea set her mom had gotten at a garage sale. Maddy did love setting it up and serving tea to her stuffed animals.

"Come on, Maddy. Time to go." She ran a comb through Maddy's black curls and kissed her chubby little cheek.

They piled into her car and drove toward the main lodge, about a half mile away. Parking and getting out, they were blasted by the sounds of a live country band. She spotted Hunter Sullivan as they neared the party, and waved, very glad to see a friendly face.

He nodded his head at her and walked toward them. "Hey, Kelsey. Who's this little angel?" He tugged on one of Maddy's dark curls, and she instantly giggled.

"Hi, Hunter. This is Maddy. And my mother, Bunny Randolph."

"Ma'am, pleased to meet you." He tipped his hat at her mother, then took Maddy's tiny hand in his own. "And Miss Maddy, it's a real honor to meet you. Will you save a dance for me?"

Maddy giggled again and buried her face in Kelsey's shoulder. But before long, she peeked out at him again.

Why you little flirt. You take after Grandma, don't you? But then, who can resist a cowboy like Hunter? He certainly was good-looking, and his green eyes sparkled back at her daughter. Definitely a charmer.

Turning around, she looked for Nash, finally spotting him in the shadows. He seemed to be staring at someone. Or more accurately, shooting daggers at them.

"Hunter, who is that over by the speakers?"

He glanced up, then frowned. "That's Mindy and her husband, Ben. She and Nash dated in college. Till Ben stole her from him. They never come to these parties." He made a sound of disapproval, his frown deepening. "Why now?"

"Is he still hung up on her?"

"Nah. I think he's more pissed he lost his best friend than her."

"They can't still be friends?"

He shrugged. "Nash hasn't gone out much—actually at all—since he's been home." He frowned once more, then smiled at her and patted his flat stomach. "I'm hungry. Let's go eat."

They walked to the buffet tables set up near the dance floor. Something roasted on a spit, and the tantalizing aroma made her mouth water. The table was lined with bowl after bowl of salads, from green to three kinds of potato, and pasta salads. Baskets filled to overflowing with buns and rolls were next, then chips and dips. She groaned, wanting to try everything. A carving station with several types of meats sat apart from the buffet line, and she spotted a staggering array of red meat and barbecued chicken.

Nash's father had explained that while this was a guest ranch, they were also a working cattle ranch.

"Mommy, cake!"

She looked to see Maddy pointing at two more tables loaded with desserts: cakes, pies, cookies and a portable soft-serve ice-cream machine. The Sullivans sure knew how to throw a party.

"Come on and sit with me," Hunter said, leading the way to one of the picnic tables.

Not long after they'd started eating, three men and

a little boy joined them at the table. Each one set their plates down, then tipped their cowboy hats at her and her mother.

"Kelsey, Bunny and Maddy, these are my brothers. Kade and his son, Toby. Wyatt is the ugly one with the long hair in the middle. Luke at the end of the table."

A chorus of "ma'am's" echoed all around, and Kelsey was a little overwhelmed at the sheer testosterone flooding the air. Every one of them was tall, dark and really, did they *all* have to be so ruggedly good-looking?

Bunny preened. "My goodness. I can't believe one of you big strapping young men is Kelsey's patient."

"Mom…"

"No, ma'am. That would be Nash, our oldest brother," Wyatt spoke up.

"Is he here tonight?" her mother asked.

"Probably around somewhere." Hunter picked up his fork.

"Uncle Hunter, did you bring the triples?" Toby asked.

Kelsey looked at Toby, a young miniature of his father, with coal-black hair and big blue eyes. *Triples?*

Hunter shook his head. "Nope," he said, frowning. "Their mother took them to see her parents."

"Who or what are *triples*?" she asked.

Hunter grinned. "That's what Toby calls my sons. They're triplets, six years old." He pulled his cell phone out and pulled up a picture of them.

Three identical faces stared up at her, all mugging for the camera, hanging all over Hunter, who looked like he adored them.

"They're adorable. When will your wife be back with them?"

"That'd be ex-wife."

"Oh, I'm sorry."

"I'm not. We were in college, she got pregnant, we married, had the boys. But realized we were better off apart. She lives in Billings and we share custody."

Hunter had befriended her from the instant they met. Tonight she got to know the other two brothers a little better. Luke, the veterinarian for the ranch, kept them all laughing with stories about some of his run-ins with large animals. He had a quick wit and a ready smile, and she had a feeling he didn't lack for female companionship.

Wyatt, on the other hand, didn't say much. Some kind of pain lurked behind his hazel eyes. Just like the other men, he was cowboy handsome, although his hair was much longer than the others. But there was an edge to him, a roughness, and it made her wonder what had happened in his past.

Everyone had secrets, which of course made her think about Nash. She picked at her food, kind of hoping he would join them.

As the sky darkened, the white twinkling lights glowed like stars above the party, and the dancing started. The Sullivan brothers started peeling away, and her mother chatted with another couple at the next table.

A short time later, Kelsey excused herself and went to the main lodge to use the restroom. As she walked down the hall following the signs to the ladies' room, she peeked into the big open room, astonished at the vaulted ceilings crisscrossed by beams worn dark over time. This room, too, had a wall of glass that faced the mountains and lake. The place was luxurious without being ostentatious, and definitely had a Western flair with dark colors, plaids and big comfy furniture.

After washing her hands, she left the bathroom and headed back outside. Nash's voice stopped her, and she looked around for him. She sneaked a quick glance around the corner of the lodge and saw him talking to the couple Hunter had mentioned to her earlier. It wasn't polite to eavesdrop, and she knew she should move, but was afraid they'd hear her.

"We were so sorry to hear about you getting hurt over there, Nash," the blonde woman said.

"Thanks."

"You doing any better now?" The man clapped a hand on Nash's shoulder.

"I'm all right."

"I noticed you walking with a limp—you sure you're okay?"

"I said I'm fine, Mindy." Nash nodded once and looked at the ground.

"Oh, well…" She turned and snuggled up to her husband. "Did I tell you my Ben is now president of the bank?"

"Is he? Then I guess congrats are in order. Looks like you ended up with the better man."

Mindy giggled. "I sure did! I just love my big, strong, handsome man."

Kelsey winced, and her heart hurt for Nash. Even as she watched, he withdrew into himself and stepped back, his bad leg dragging in the dust.

"I need to go check on something. Congratulations again, Ben. See you." He turned and headed away from them.

The other couple wandered back toward the party, and Kelsey stood there, trying to decide if she should follow Nash or leave him alone. His state of mind right now was critical to the therapy process. *Oh sure. That's why I want to check on him—it has nothing to do with wanting to get closer to this ornery, attractive cowboy.* Decision made, she hurried along the path he'd taken toward the barn.

The door stood open, and she peeked inside but couldn't see much in the dim light. She finally made out Nash standing outside one of the horse stalls, his hand resting on a horse's nose.

Seeing him like this, without his defensive posture and hot words at the ready, she hurt for him. He was a man's man, the sort whose physical abilities defined who and what he was. And right now, Nash didn't know who that was. When he rested his forehead against the horse's forelock, his defeat was heartbreaking.

The horse neighed, and nudged Nash's shoulder as if offering support.

"You wanna get the hell out of here too, Thunder?" There was no gruffness, no anger—only grief. "I wish we could."

Guilt pricked her conscience. She shouldn't be here listening to him, so she backed away, but kicked something that clanged.

"Who's there?" Nash demanded.

"It's just me. Sorry, I didn't mean to intrude."

"Why are you here?" He started walking toward her.

"Oh, um. My mother and daughter are up at the party. Do you want to come meet them?"

"I'm not the best company right now. Rain check?" Nash suddenly crashed to the ground in front of her, his foot tangled up in a heavy rope. "Dammit!" he exploded, kicking at the rope.

A high-pitched giggle echoed on the wind outside the barn, and Kelsey stuck her head out the door. Mindy and Ben were headed straight back on a path to the barn. She turned, saw him still struggling to get up. Hurrying over, she knelt down to untangle the rope, but in her haste, she made it worse.

"I can do it," he snapped, shoving her hand away.

High-pitched giggles floated again, and she reacted. Fast. She swung a leg over his waist and straddled him, sinking down on top of him.

Her move cut him off midcurse, and he stopped, staring up at her, his mouth open. "What the—"

"They're coming." She bent forward and latched her lips on his.

He pushed her shoulders up. "What the hell?"

"Just shut up and kiss me."

He stared up at her as another giggle floated around the corner of the barn. She bent over again and kissed him.

It was the only thing she could think of to save his pride.

His head tilted sideways, and he kissed her back. And oh God, did he ever kiss her back. His lips were just a little rough, and they scraped across her mouth, devouring it. Tingles shot down her spine, up her legs, and swung around to pool in her lower belly.

Maybe this isn't such a good idea.

She hadn't been with anyone since Rob died. Didn't *want* to be with anyone. But this... God, she'd forgotten how good it could be when two people were attracted to each other.

But Nash and I aren't attracted to each other. He's my client. Period.

"Oh! Excuse us."

A high-pitched voice barely penetrated the fog in her brain. She started to pull away from Nash, but he tightened his hold, slid his hands around her back. One hand drifted down her spine, and he dipped his fingers beneath her shirt, teasing her bare skin.

"I *said*, excuse us."

Kelsey slowly sat up, staring at Nash.

He drifted his thumb over her lower lip, and the tingles raced again down her spine. Tilting his head to look around her, he said, "Guess we got a little tangled up in each other." His voice was all rough, sexy cowboy now, and it did something to her insides.

He looked up at her again and grinned.

She smiled back, oddly pleased he'd included her in an inside joke about getting tangled up.

This is just fake. It doesn't mean anything... Rob. Think of Rob.

Yet her body had come alive in Nash's arms, her blood racing, awakening feelings she hadn't had since she'd buried her husband. She started to climb off him, but he held her in place, so that her most tender spot was right over the growing bulge in his jeans.

HE HELD KELSEY so she couldn't scramble off him just yet. She was the perfect shield to get rid of two people he didn't want to talk to again. And she felt good against him. Too good. He hadn't been with a woman in a long time. Too long, if the way he'd hardened almost instantly when she kissed him was any indicator.

She stared down at him, her long dark hair hanging down to brush his chest. God, he wished he didn't have a shirt on so he could feel it. So far he'd only seen it in a braid and hadn't noticed how long and silky it was. He wanted to tangle his hands in her hair, draw her down and kiss her over and over.

"Nash," she hissed, and tried to get up again.

"Stay, babe. They'll leave if we just ignore 'em." At least he hoped they would, and before she gave in to the panic starting to bloom on her face.

"Well, how rude," said Mindy. "But then you never were much of a gentleman."

Kelsey turned her head toward Mindy and Ben. "Some women don't want a gentleman all the time."

He looked up at her, shocked at the sexy words. She actually looked pretty shocked, too.

Glancing around Kelsey, he saw Mindy's face go red. Ben put an arm around her. "Come on, sweetie. Let's leave them alone. You still owe me a dance."

The minute the other couple was out of sight, Kelsey scrambled off him and stood, then extended a hand to him. "Come on, cowboy. I need to get back to my mom and daughter."

He took her hand, slowly testing his balance. Once he was stable on his feet, he tried to catch her eye. "Thank you."

She looked up at him. "I'm sorry. I shouldn't have done that."

"Why did you?"

"I don't know. Hunter said something about them, and…" She shrugged. "I knew you wouldn't want them, or anyone, to see you on the ground."

"Without a good reason, at least." He grinned.

Pink suffused her cheeks, and she turned away.

"Seriously. Thanks." Her earlier words registered, and he frowned. "You said before you have a daughter. I assume you have a husband, too. I don't want him to hear about this and think I'm moving in on his wife."

"I'm a widow," she said, so quietly he had to bend closer to hear the words.

"Ah, geez. I'm sorry. What happened?"

"Accident."

"How long?"

"Almost three years."

"That's rough. Do you—"

"I have to go." She started off at a fast clip, then

swung around. "Just know I normally don't do that type of thing."

"What type of thing?"

"Throw myself at men."

She rushed off before he could say anything else.

A cold shower sounded good right now. He needed to cool off, even if she was only pretending for his sake. His steps slowed even further. She'd done it to save his pride. Rubbing a hand across his stubbled chin, he caught a whiff of something light, feminine. Sniffing his fingertips, he groaned.

Kelsey's perfume.

Everything had happened so fast he hadn't really paid attention before. Now it was embedded in his nose, and it brought back the feeling of her sitting across his groin. He hadn't been *that* turned on in, well…forever.

His leg ached and he wanted more than anything to sit down. Well, he wanted to take her to bed, but that wouldn't happen anytime soon.

With anyone.

What woman would be interested in him now?

He didn't want anyone to see him this way. Kelsey didn't count; she was a therapist. "That's all she is, and ever will be," he told himself.

Maybe if he said it often enough, he'd believe it.

The music from the band grew louder with every step he took. A sudden racket from the drums hit fever pitch, and he flinched. The rat-a-tats wouldn't stop, and he ducked, searching for cover.

Nowhere to hide…alone.

He looked at his hand. *Where's my weapon?*

Searching his pockets turned up nothing.

He needed a gun or a knife.

Something.

Anything to fight back.

A hand clamped down on his shoulder.

He wrenched his body back, out of the enemy's grip. Pulled his arm back to throw a punch.

His dad stood in front of him. "What's wrong with you? Didn't you hear me calling?"

Nash looked around the shadowed yard. Pickup trucks of all sizes lined the driveway; flowers bloomed in the gardens.

No desert. No rocks.

No one trying to kill him.

Nausea gripped his stomach, and he broke out in a clammy sweat. He needed to get back to his cabin. This hadn't ever happened before. His leg muscles threatened to seize up, and he blew out a breath, tried to lengthen his stride. His right foot hit a gopher hole, and he caught himself before he fell.

"I've been looking for you."

His dad's voice seemed to come from a tunnel, and he tried to focus on answering. "What do you want?"

"Did you get something to eat?"

"I'm not hungry."

"I didn't see you up there. Come back and say hello to everyone."

"No."

"Why the hell not? They're our guests, and they all know you. Want to see the returning hero." His dad clapped him on the back.

A growl erupted from deep within, and he jerked his shoulder away from his dad's hand, stepped back. "I'm no hero." Sweat beaded on his forehead, dampened his palms. He needed to get out of there, and now.

"You get yourself back up to the party and play nice."

His dad stepped closer and peered at Nash's face. "What's wrong with you?"

"Leave me alone." He did hurry this time, all the way to his truck. He'd thought earlier he could suck it up and go to the barbecue.

Not now.

He pulled out of the parking area, the headlights flashing across his dad. Nash's chest tightened. Was that concern on the old man's face?

Nah. Impossible.

KELSEY STOOD ON the edge of the dance floor watching Hunter dance with Maddy. He whirled her around, and she hooted with laughter.

She smiled. It was good to see her daughter having fun.

"Maddy sure is taken with Hunter, isn't she?" her mother remarked.

"She definitely is."

"Why aren't *you* taken with Hunter?"

Suppressing an eye roll, Kelsey said, "Because I don't want to be taken with any man. I don't have time for nonsense."

"But you're still young and vital—"

"Mother, stop it."

"I'm just saying, the Sullivans seem to be doing well for themselves. I used the Google earlier to look at their guest ranch, and all the reviews are five star. Wouldn't hurt to make an effort."

"I had a husband, and he died. I don't think…no, I know I'll never love anyone that way again."

"Who said anything about love? What about security? Having someone to turn to at night? Not being alone again."

Kelsey slid her arm around her mother's shoulder. "I know you miss Dad."

"Nonsense. I was talking about you."

Reaching deep for patience, Kelsey cut her words off when Nash's father stopped in front of them.

"Kelsey, I'm glad you came tonight. I wanted to officially welcome you to the Sullivan Ranch." His words were for Kelsey, but he hadn't taken his eyes off her mother. "Who's this lovely woman with you?" he asked, and took his Stetson off even as he sucked in his stomach.

Bunny preened and fluffed her blond hair. "Why, how kind of you, Mr. Sullivan. I'm Bunny Randolph, Kelsey's mother." She drew out all the syrupy sugar of her Southern upbringing as she spoke.

Mr. Sullivan took her hand in his and pressed a kiss to the back of it. "It's a pleasure meetin' you, ma'am. Just call me Angus. Both of you."

Kelsey stood next to them, trying hard not to laugh. Bunny was pouring on the Southern charm, and Mr. Sullivan pulled out his inner cowboy.

He pressed her hand into the crook of his elbow just as the band slowed the tempo down into a Tennessee waltz. "May I have the pleasure of this dance?"

"I thought you'd never ask." Her mother's voice had gone breathless, and she put an extra swish into her skirts as they walked away, completely ignoring Kelsey.

"Seems I'm not the only one taken with your family." Hunter joined her, carrying a sleepy Madison.

She took her daughter in her arms, and Maddy tucked her head against her shoulder. Her arms strained with the weight, and she tightened her grip, hating that her daughter was growing up so fast. And Rob wouldn't be there to watch.

"I better get her home. Do you think someone could bring my mom home after the party?"

"Don't worry. I'll take her home. Although—" he broke off and glanced toward the dance floor "—my dad may beat me to it. They seem to be gettin' along pretty good."

Angus twirled her mom around the floor, then dipped her. Bunny squealed and laughed, beaming up at him.

There she goes, flirting again. On the one hand, she needed this job, but on the other, she needed to get Nash up to speed so they could move on before Bunny got too attached. Again. She drew men to her like bees to honeysuckle, and she loved it.

"You go on ahead and take your daughter home. I'll make sure your mom is fine. Sleep tight." He kissed her cheek, then smoothed a gentle hand down Maddy's back.

"Thanks, Hunter. I appreciate you doing that. And for keeping Maddy entertained. She loved dancing with you. Good night."

Once she had Maddy buckled into the car seat, she leaned against the driver door and looked up at the sky. There had to be more than a billion stars. She'd never seen so many, or so clearly. Montana could definitely grow on her. Not humid at all like back home in Florida. No lights, except from the ranch. Inhaling a deep breath, she smelled nothing but clean air, hay and wood smoke.

A cow mooed not too far away, followed by a coyote's long undulating howl. Chills snaked down her back, and she climbed into the car quickly and started it, making a mental note to make sure Maddy never went outside alone.

Once she'd reached the cabin and gotten her daughter settled, she made a cup of tea and carried it to the porch. She sank into one of the rocking chairs and sipped.

What a perfect night. Well, perfectly confusing. Memories of the episode with Nash crashed into her mind, and her blood ran hot. "Why the heck did I do that? He's a grown-ass man, doesn't need me to come to his rescue," she muttered.

"So why did you?"

She shrieked and bolted from the chair, dropping the mug, and it smashed on the wooden floorboards. A shadow detached from the corner of her cabin, and Nash appeared in the dim light shining out the window.

"Don't do that!" she snapped at him.

"Do what?"

"Sneak up on me and appear out of the darkness."

"I figured you'd have heard me coming a mile away."

"Well, I didn't," she griped, looking at the ruins of her favorite mug on the floorboards.

"I guess you were too busy castigating yourself to pay attention to the hitch in my gitalong."

A laugh burst out before she could stop it. In fact, she couldn't stop laughing and had to bend double to catch her breath.

"What in tarnation are you laughing about?"

She plopped down in the rocking chair and wiped her eyes. "I can't quite figure you out. One minute you're twanging up your speech with cowboyisms, then you go and use *castigate*."

The light caught his face as he frowned. "I'm not a hick. I may not have graduated from college—"

"That's not what I meant at all. Your dad came up to us at the party and he pretty much did the same thing when I introduced him to my mom."

The scowl on his face deepened, and he muttered something under his breath.

"I didn't hear you."

"I said he's always been a flirt, even before my mom died."

She sobered instantly, uncomfortable. "I'm sorry."

He shook his head. "Never mind. Forget I said anything."

She picked at a loose thread on her shirt. "So why are you out here? Checking up on us?"

"Now why would I do that? You're a grown-ass woman, ain't ya?" The corner of his mouth lifted as he threw the words back at her.

"Ha ha. Why are you here?"

"Couldn't sleep, needed some air. Forgot this was the cabin my dad put you in." He pushed off from the post he'd been leaning against, looked around. "Y'all settle in okay?"

"We're just fine. It's a gorgeous cabin. Hard to believe something like this is out in the middle of nowhere. I'm surprised it was sitting empty and not snatched up by some tourist."

"Plenty of cabins to go around."

"It's an amazing ranch. I've always thought dude ranches were small, with rickety, dusty cabins and city slickers wanting to experience a cattle roundup."

"It used to be that way. But my mom was a dreamer, and she wanted to build this place up into a five-star guest ranch. So, here we are."

"How come you left here, joined the Army?" His shoulders tightened, and she almost regretted asking him, but the question had been rolling around her head all evening.

He shrugged. "Restless, I guess."

"I get restless, I take up a new hobby, or go on a trip. Joining the Army is pretty drastic."

"College wasn't doing it for me, and Dad and I kept

butting heads, so, I left." He shifted, leaning against the railing. "Did y'all have a good time tonight?"

"Yup. Maddy had a blast dancing with Hunter."

He grinned. "He's got a way with kids. Has three of his own."

She laughed. "The triples. I got a kick out of Toby's name for them."

"They're good kids. So's Toby." He looked up, and she followed his gaze to the stars.

The longer he stood there silent, the more she wondered why he seemed to be drawing out his visit. "Do you need anything? How's your leg?"

He glared at her, the corner of his lip curling up. "I'm fine," he said, his words clipped. "'Night." He walked away, his limp more pronounced.

Instead of calling after him, she bit her tongue. He wouldn't appreciate her treating him like an invalid. Best just to leave him alone.

But now she knew what he tasted like.

Felt like.

How could her body know his so quickly?

Crave it?

Chapter Four

Several days later, after a grueling session with Kelsey, Nash had snapped at her to leave him alone. All he wanted was a soak in a cool tub. But he needed to be outdoors, not cooped up in his cabin. His mind flashed to the pond where he used to go skinny-dipping. The cool water would feel good on this abnormally warm July day.

He grabbed a towel and climbed into the truck, his leg aching like a sonovabitch. He drove to the hidden spot, cursing a blue streak. Good thing his momma couldn't hear him now, or she'd take a spatula to his backside. He'd loved her a lot, and it nearly broke him when she died. He'd only been ten, and Hunter was barely a year old, with the other three ranging in age between them. No-nonsense, good Christian, but a lot of fun. The light left their house that day.

Seeing the split in the trees that led to the pond, he pulled over and parked. Out of all his brothers, he'd been the only one to consider it his sanctuary. Why hadn't he come back here before now?

He tried to get out of the truck, and had to lift his left leg out. Yeah, that was why. Damn leg.

Throwing his Stetson on the dashboard, he slammed the door, then picked his way across the uneven ground. About a hundred feet through the trees, the path opened up to sparkling blue water. He wanted in that pond so bad he could taste it. Yanking off his T-shirt, he threw it on the flat rock that sat a few feet up from the water. Leaning against it, the trapped warmth heated his backside, and he stripped off his jeans as fast as he could. Hauling himself onto the flat rock wasn't as easy as he'd hoped, but he made it.

A flash of light blinded him for a minute, and he realized it was the sun glinting off his leg. He punched the prosthesis, and was rewarded with stinging knuckles.

Rustling from the bushes about six yards to the left caught his attention, and he squinted in the sunlight. Didn't see anything. Probably some animal coming for water. As long as it wasn't a bear or a mountain lion, he didn't care. Unwrapping the binding on the leg, he pulled it off, held it up in the air, tempted to pitch it into the pond.

A bloodcurdling scream split the quiet afternoon, scaring him so much he almost fell off the rock. He looked around for a predator crouching to attack. Standing near the water's edge was a little girl with dark curly hair.

Screaming.

He froze. What the hell should he do? He was naked, holding a fake leg in the air, with a little girl screaming bloody murder. He grabbed his T-shirt and clamped it to his privates.

"It's okay. I won't hurt you. Who are you?"

The screaming continued, and he knew she hadn't heard him.

He tried to fit his leg back into place, but his hands shook so bad this time he really did almost drop it into the water.

"Maddy! Madison!" a woman's frantic voice called.

Kelsey? A light dawned and he realized this must be her daughter.

"It's okay, Madison. I know your mommy." His words were still drowned out by her voice. Her very loud voice.

"Maddy! What is it? Are you hurt?" Kelsey stumbled through another break in the trees. She knelt down in front of the girl and frantically checked her over. "Sweetie, what's wrong? I can't help you if you don't tell me."

The little girl's screams subsided into gulping sobs, and she pointed at him.

Even though he was a few yards away, he saw Kelsey freeze, prepared to pounce on whatever threatened her daughter. She grabbed a thick stick next to her, leaped to her feet and whirled around to face him.

"Nash?" she asked, looking around the perimeter of the pond.

He waved. "Hiya."

"Um…is there a wild animal here?"

"Nope."

"Why is my daughter screaming?"

He held up his leg. "I was getting ready to swi—"

Maddy screamed again, Kelsey dropped the stick and picked her up. She walked several feet away and turned around so the girl wasn't facing him anymore.

This was the damn reason he didn't want to be around people. Ever again. They'd see him as a freak. He'd come home to prove he was still the same person.

But even a little girl knew he wasn't.

He started to climb down, then realized he was still naked. Looking up to ask Kelsey to leave, he could tell she'd just realized he was naked, too. Color swept up her neck, then her face, until she looked like a sun-ripened strawberry. Her eyes widened as she stared at him, her tongue darting out to lick her lower lip.

He hardened instantly and hunched over, trying to hide it with the T-shirt. How could one look from her turn him on so much? Even when she was trying to calm her daughter down? Glancing at the water, he knew he needed to get in there. Fast. Or he'd embarrass both of them to no end.

He looked up to ask her to leave, but didn't see either of them. *Great.* He dropped the leg on the rock, wincing as it hit the granite with a clang. Scooting to the edge, he lowered himself into the water, grateful for the freezing runoff from the glacier that fed into the stream, filling his pond.

Scanning the area once more, he was satisfied they were gone. Letting himself go, he floated, the sun heating his front, and the water cooling his back. His muscles relaxed, bit by bit, and the pain in his leg reduced to random twinges.

He let the cold water soothe his aches. If only it could soothe the noise in his head. Squinching his eyes closed, he still heard the little girl's screams echo in his brain. She'd been terrified of him. Without even opening his eyes, he knew he looked like a monster. Between the white scars against his tanned skin, and no leg—no wonder the poor kid had screamed.

Great reinforcement for not having kids. Not that any woman would want him anyway. He didn't want to mentally scar the kids he used to want, and hoped Madison would forget what she'd seen an hour ago.

Maybe I can just stay here, never leave this place. A flash of Kelsey's blue eyes squinting at him as she pushed him in rehab made him think she'd just hunt him down here so she could torture him some more. "Screw her," he mumbled.

And of course those words made him think about what it would be like to do that to her literally. Not that she'd let him. But considering the way his body reacted just thinking about her, he could at least fantasize in case he needed to take matters into his own hand. The cold water wasn't helping right now, and he cupped himself, wishing...

"I wanted to apol—"

He jackknifed up, then his foot slipped off a rock, and he went underwater. Thrashing around for balance, he rose up for air, coughing up the water he'd swallowed.

Kelsey stood at the edge of the pond, her hands plastered over her eyes. From what little he could see of her cheeks, they were blazing red.

Great. Just great. Did she actually see me...?

"Why'd you come back? Where's Maddy?" he asked, moving his arms back and forth for balance, trying to stay upright.

She lowered her hands to look at him. "She's with my mother back at the car. We finished our picnic and I wanted to say I'm sorry for Maddy's—" Her hands flew up again to cover her eyes.

"What's wrong?"

"That's really clear water in the pond there. Did you know that?"

"Sure. The water all over the ranch is like this."

"You can see every rock, every plant, real clear." She still hadn't lowered her hands.

He looked down and saw everything magnified in the waist-deep water. Dammit. He started swimming, or trying to, and ended up practically dog-paddling to the edge. The rock ledge loomed over him, and he reached to pull himself up. It had been a long time since he'd been to the pond, and he'd forgotten that to get out, he needed to push off. With his legs.

"Uh, Kelsey?"

"Yes," she answered, still covering her eyes.

"I need a hand to get out."

"Oh."

He waited, could almost see the wheels turning in her head.

"Maybe we could turn this into a session." She peeked out through her fingers, he assumed to assess the rock, shoreline and find a way he could get out.

"Just get me out of here," he growled.

"You're going to have to learn how to do this on your own if you come back here. Might as well start today."

"Get me the hell out of this pond. Don't lecture me about rehab. I can't get out by myself. You think that makes me happy?" If she said one more damn word about rehab, he wouldn't be responsible for his actions.

"Fine," she huffed, dropping her hands to her sides. She stomped to the edge and held her hand out.

He reached up to grab her hand, and she pulled. Using his foot, he tried to scramble as best he could up the slippery slope.

She gripped his wrist with her other hand and pulled again, just as he started sliding backward. He tried to let go, but she followed him with a big splash and sank underwater. She rose to the surface, spluttering and coughing.

"Kelsey, I'm so sorry. I didn't mean—"

Her outrage was so absolute he was surprised the water didn't start boiling around them. Her black as sin hair plastered to her head, and she scooped it out of her eyes.

A tickle rose up his throat, and he tried to cough it back. Which only made it worse. It turned into a snort.

"You did that on purpose, didn't you?" The accusatory finger aimed his way could have been a lethal weapon.

Choking back another laugh, he held his hands up. "No, ma'am. Honestly, I didn't."

Her eyes narrowed, and she swiped a hand down her face. "Better not have, mister," she muttered, heading for the shore.

Another laugh bubbled up, and it felt so foreign, he let it out. Which was followed by another laugh, sounding rusty even to his ears.

She froze and slowly turned to face him. Drawing her hand back, she swooshed it across the surface, sending a tidal wave of water into his face.

It should have pissed him off, but even as he coughed out the water, he admired her feistiness.

Reaching the shore a few yards from the rocky ledge, she turned around to wait for him. "Hurry up. I need to get packed up and back to the cabin for Maddy's nap."

He swam forward, cursing himself for being naked.

"The bank is more of a gentle slope here. I'll put my arm around you, and you lean on me however much you need to."

God, he hated this. Having to depend on someone to help him grated on every last nerve. And to rely on a woman, any woman, made it worse.

Her hand slid across his back and around his side as she tried to support him, leaving a trail of fire over his slick skin. *Oh geez. Think of something else. Anything else besides her hand on me.* He pictured the pile of horse manure he'd had to shovel as punishment one hot summer as a teenager just to get him the few yards till he could grab his towel.

He tried not to pant as they hobbled together out of the water. Hated showing weakness, even if she was a therapist. As soon as they were close enough, he leaned forward and grabbed his towel off the rock, wrapped it around his waist. "Thanks."

"You're welcome." Her voice sounded breathless, and he glanced up to see her hurrying away. She stopped suddenly. "You okay from here?" she asked without turning around.

"Yeah."

Leaves crunched as she hurried away, leaving him alone with the crickets. He dried off, then leaned against the rock, looked around the serene setting. This place had always been his sanctuary, a place to be completely alone.

And now it would always remind him of limitations.

And desperate need.

Chapter Five

Kelsey couldn't settle down, even hours later, after catching Nash in the pond.

Naked.

Scars notwithstanding, his body was perfection. Muscles that in no way came from a gym curved under tight, tanned skin. Even with the scars, he was perfect.

And not someone she should be thinking of in this way. He was her patient.

She'd had her happiness before, even with the heartache. Didn't want to be with another man. Couldn't take that chance. Not with her heart, or her daughter's.

Her mother rushed into the living room. "Are you ready? Is Maddy ready? I don't want to keep Angus waiting."

"Mom, calm down. We're all ready to go." They'd been invited to dinner with the family at Angus's house that night. She wondered how much of that invite was finagling on her mother's part, and how much came from Angus being smitten with Bunny.

She grabbed her mother's hand, hoping to instill some reality. "Mom, you know we won't be here all that long."

"I know, pumpkin. But can't we make friends while we're here?"

Suppressing an eye roll, Kelsey packed up Maddy and

her bag of toys, and they all piled in her car. She turned the key, heard nothing but grinding. *Please, not now. Behave till I can save up some money!*

She switched the ignition key off, waited a beat, tried again. This time it groaned to life, protesting the whole way.

Reaching the main lodge a short time later, they were invited inside by a beaming Angus. She scanned the big rustic living room, really hoping Nash wasn't in attendance. She had the feeling from something Hunter had said at the barbecue that Nash didn't do many family things since he'd been discharged from the Army.

"Glad y'all could make it tonight," Angus said.

"It was nice of you to invite us."

He pulled her aside, away from the laughter of his sons. "How's my son doing with therapy?"

"We're working hard every day. He's really coming along." At least she hoped so, at this point.

"Good. You let me know if he gives you any trouble."

She just smiled, knowing she'd never go to him, and took the glass of wine the housekeeper gave her.

The front door opened, and Wyatt walked in. "I had to pretty much hog-tie him, but he's here for family night." He stepped aside as Nash walked in, scowling.

Nash met her eyes, and stopped short, his grimace turning even scarier.

Angus stepped forward and took Bunny's arm. "Nash, this is Bunny Randolph, Kelsey's mother. I don't think you met the other night."

Nash tipped his head and shook her mother's hand. "Nice meeting you, ma'am."

"My goodness, Angus. You have such a handsome family!" her mother said, and tucked her hand beneath

Angus's elbow. "You're so lucky the boys all still live here."

He preened. "We try to do a family dinner at least once a month. Now we're all here except for Luke. He's gone to an auction in Vegas."

"Mommy, look!" Maddy ran into the room holding a small cowboy hat. Kelsey saw the instant she noticed Nash. Her face crumpled and she started crying.

Hunter hurried over to her and swung Maddy up into his arms. "Shh, shh, shh. It's okay, honey. Did that big bad man scare you?" He tucked Maddy's head into his shoulder, muffling her sobs. The look he threw at Nash was part concern, part *what'd you go and do now?*

Kelsey glanced at Nash and was shocked at the heartbroken look on his face. He raised his head and looked at her, and the pain disappeared behind a mask. His boots thumped on the wood floor as he backtracked and went out the front door, closing it behind him.

She started to follow, but Hunter brought Maddy to her. "I think she wants you." She took her daughter into her arms and cuddled her, relieved when the crying jag ended quickly.

"I should go after Nash, make sure he's okay," she whispered to Hunter.

"Why? He'll be fine. Maddy just hasn't met him yet."

Kelsey swallowed the words, wanting to tell him what had happened earlier, and how Nash had to be hurting. It wasn't her place to tell his family about the real reason he was out of the Army now.

Hours later, after a wonderful dinner, she drove her mother and Maddy home. While she'd had a good time and liked getting to know the Sullivan men, she couldn't stop worrying about Nash. Once they were settled, she told her mother she was going out for a walk and would be back soon. Not wanting to risk her car, she set out on foot to Nash's cabin, the flashlight app on her phone guiding the way.

The lights were off at his cabin, and she'd just about decided not to wake him up when she noticed the rocking chair on the porch lying on its side. The night was calm with the occasional soft breeze. Nothing strong enough to knock over a chair. Darkness shrouded the cabin, but light flickered beyond the open door.

If he was asleep, she should do the neighborly thing and close it for him so no critters would get in during the night.

She walked softly to the door and peeked inside. Holding her cell phone up, she shined her light around the big room to make sure no animals had already gotten in. The TV was on, casting an eerie glow across a mess. She gasped and felt around the wall for the light switch. Flicking it on, chills exploded in her stomach.

Nothing had been left untouched. Furniture was scattered all over the room, pictures flung off the walls, dirt from an overturned planter showed footprints tracked through it. The trophies that had been on the bookcase were on the floor. It looked like someone had taken a hammer and dented every single one, trying to destroy them.

"Nash! Are you here? Are you okay?"

Hesitating in case the intruder was still there, concern finally overrode her fear and propelled her forward to search for him. The bedroom door stood wide-open, and she flicked on the light. The sheets had been thrown back, and shards from the mirror over the dresser lay in jagged pieces across the floor to mix with a smashed bottle.

"Where are you?" she muttered. Back in the main room, she walked around the island separating the kitchen and den, and came across more broken glass by the sink. Empty bottles of whiskey, it looked like.

But no Nash.

"Okay, think. Call the cops?" Realizing it wasn't her place to call the cops, she dialed Hunter instead.

He answered on the fourth ring, sounding groggy. "Kelsey? You okay?"

"I walked over to Nash's cabin to make sure he's okay, and I can't find him."

"He'll be fine. Probably out walking."

"I think something's wrong. The front door was open, and every room is a mess. Either he did this, or someone broke in."

Hunter muttered a curse word. "I'll be there in a minute."

As she waited, she debated about cleaning up what she could. But in case someone *had* broken in, she thought she'd better leave it alone.

Hunter walked in a few minutes later only to stop short and whistle. "You weren't kidding, were you?" His short dark brown hair stuck up at all angles, and he ran a hand over it.

She shook her head. "I wish I was," she said, and wrapped her hands together to stop the trembling.

"I took a look outside first. His truck is gone. If he did this, I know where he might have gone. I'll need reinforcements, though." He pulled his cell phone out and dialed. "Kade, Nash is missing. Kelsey and I think something's wrong, and he might be at Smokey Joe's." He hung up the phone. "Kade's calling Wyatt, and I'll meet them in town."

"What's Smokey Joe's?"

"A bar."

"Okay. Let's go."

He held up a hand. "Wait a minute. You don't need to go."

"The heck I don't. I want to make sure he's okay. I'm going, and you can't stop me."

He studied her. "You sure that's all you want to do? Why so concerned?"

Heat suffused her face. "He's my patient. Now stop wasting time. No telling how long he's been there."

But was that all it was? Concern for her patient?

She shook her head. *Can't think about that now.*

Even though he was driving above the speed limit, Kelsey wanted to urge Hunter to go faster. But in the darkness, with the chance of wild animals wandering across the road, she bit her tongue. *Please be okay, please be okay*, she prayed the whole way to town.

Reaching the town limits, Hunter slowed the truck and wove his way through empty streets until turning into a parking lot filled with pickup trucks and motorcycles.

She glanced at her watch, surprised it was already well past midnight, and the place was lit up like Christmas. Hunter parked just as Kade and Wyatt got out of a truck and waited for them at the front door.

"Yup, he's here all right. His truck is across the street," Wyatt said, pointing to it. "How're we gonna play this?"

"What do you mean 'play this'? Let's just go get him," she fumed, anxious to see if he was okay, and why his cabin looked like a war zone. He was her patient, so she had a professional responsibility to him. *It's not personal—it's business. Right?*

"He's done this before. Won't appreciate us coming to get him."

"Men. Stupid, pigheaded, egotistical, morons." She didn't care if it chapped his ass from here to Alaska, he shouldn't be in a place like this. Grabbing the door handle, she flung it open. The stench of too many bodies, cigarettes and booze washed over her, and her head reeled. Breathing lightly through her mouth, she tried to scan the room, but the crowd dwarfed her.

A raucous cheer sounded over the twangy country song and shook the rafters. Glancing at the bartender, she saw him standing behind the bar, pulling taps, paying no attention to whatever was going on. She pushed through the crowd, looking for Nash, her shoes sticking to the floor with every step. At the back of the bar, a wall of bodies blocked her view. The sound of flesh on flesh hit her ears, and she shoved her way forward.

Finally breaking through the crowd into an open space, she almost threw up. Nash's body hung between two of the biggest, scariest men she'd ever seen. The amount of leather and piercings alone should be breaking some kind of law. A third man, even bigger, stood in front of Nash, readying to throw another punch. Blood dripped from Nash's nose and mouth, and one of his eyes was swollen shut.

She raced forward and slammed into the attacker. He was so big she barely budged him, but at least he hadn't swung at Nash again.

"What the—!" The bruiser swung around, ham-like hands fisted and ready to strike.

"Get away from him," she growled, ready to tear into the guy.

"You think *you're* gonna keep me from teaching this asshole a lesson? Although…" He leered, looking her up and down. "I'd be willin' ta teach you another kinda lesson if you wait a minute." He ran a big hand down her arm.

She smiled, and his friends cat-called and cheered,

even as she grabbed his thumb and yanked it back till he dropped to his knees, howling.

The two guys holding Nash dropped him and advanced on her. Someone brushed her shoulder, and she turned around, ready to punch. Kade, Wyatt and Hunter were lined up behind her, hands fisted and ready to protect her.

"Awright, break it up." The bartender came into view, holding a baseball bat. "You three—" he gestured at the Sullivan brothers "—get him outta here. He's caused enough trouble tonight. I don't need no more from you." He glanced at the burly guy on the floor, still cradling his hand. "And take your warrior princess with you." He winked at her.

"I'll get the truck, meet you out back," Hunter said, and left.

She hurried to Nash where he knelt on the floor, head drooping. "You okay?"

He didn't move, so she tried again. "Nash, honey? Can you hear me?"

His head moved that time, and he cracked an eye at her. "Kelsey?" He slumped forward, and she caught him, held him tight.

Kade and Wyatt moved in, and somehow they got him out the back door. She followed, relieved to see Hunter waiting inside his truck. She needed to assess Nash's injuries, but wanted to get him far away from there first. She got in and scooted to the middle of the bench seat. Wyatt helped Nash get in next to her, and she buckled him in.

Hunter started the truck and leaned forward to look at Nash. "Hey, man, if you need to puke, tell me and I'll stop. Don't hurl on my floorboards. Or on Kelsey."

Nash just grunted, his head lolling around. She shifted and cradled his head, catching a glimpse of Hunter's raised eyebrows in the side mirror. Ignoring him, she concentrated on not puking at the stench of alcohol emanating from Nash's clothes and skin. She'd probably have to burn her clothes, and maybe her shoes, considering what might have been on the floor of the bar.

Guilt and confusion swamped her. If only Maddy hadn't seen him earlier today at the pond, or tonight at the main house. Had her hysterics brought this on?

Surely Nash wouldn't let a little girl get to him this much.

Or would he?

NASH CRACKED ONE eye open, tried to open the other one, but it hurt too much. Dim light seared his eyeball, drilled right through to his brain. His stomach roiled, and a headache the likes of which he'd never had drummed through his head. He kept very still, willing himself to feel better. Didn't help.

Something jackhammered on the door, then it creaked open. "Rise and shine, sleepyhead! It's noon, time to get up," Hunter singsonged.

The words roared through his head, and he wanted to yell, but that would only make it worse. He cracked his eyelid open again, squinting against the light. Hunter leaned against the door frame, holding a cup, grinnin' like a damn fool.

"What the hell are you smilin' at?" he croaked out.

"Feel like shit, eh?" Hunter pushed off the door frame and handed Nash the cup. "Brought you some coffee and aspirin." He held out four white tablets.

Nash sat up slowly, his head weighing about two hundred pounds. He took the proffered pills and popped them into his mouth, his hand shaking. Gulping the strong black coffee, he hoped both would kick in soon. He opened his eye a bit more and looked around. "Where am I?"

"My cabin."

"Why? Did I come over last night?" He touched his aching jaw, then the puffiness around his other eye. "Did you hit me?"

"You don't remember?"

He glared at Hunter the best he could, considering he was at death's door. "Would I be asking if I remembered?"

Hunter walked over to the windows and yanked the curtains open wide. "Let's shed some light on the subject, shall we?"

Nash shut his eye against the blinding light. "I'm going to kill you once I feel better."

"What's the last thing you remember?"

Nash stayed still, racking his aching brain to try and remember the night before. Images flickered, and he tried to catch on to them. Wyatt had dragged him to family dinner night, he'd walked in the main house and the little girl started crying when she saw him. *Great. Maybe she really is traumatized now.* He'd walked out the door and kept going, all the way back to his cabin. Nothing could make him forget her screams and tears, so he'd had a drink. Then he couldn't remember anything else.

"I got to my cabin and had a drink. What'd I do?"

"You had more than one drink and must have run out. We found you at Smokey's at about one a.m."

"We?"

"Kade, Wyatt and me."

"Oh."

"And Kelsey."

His eyes flew open wide, and he winced at the ache in

his right one. "Kelsey?" Jealousy rose up, fast and bitter. Why the hell was she at a dive bar?

"She's the one who found you missing and got worried, called me." Hunter grinned. "Bartender nicknamed her 'Warrior Princess.'"

"Why?"

"She stopped some asshole from beating you up any more than he had, then dropped him to his knees when he made a pass at her."

So she wasn't out partying. His fist unclenched.

He started to grin, but his mouth hurt, and he touched his lower lip where it'd been split. Embarrassment rode fast on the heels of admiring her spirit, and shame that she saw him getting beat up. He hadn't been in a fight in a long time, not since he'd graduated boot camp and realized not everything could be solved with fists.

"She's somethin' special, isn't she?" Hunter asked.

Spots flashed in front of him, and he wanted to pummel his brother. "You interested in her?" he growled.

Hunter leaned back against the wall and crossed his arms. "I don't know…maybe," he drawled. "Think she'd go out with—"

"No," he lashed out.

"You want her for yourself?"

Yes. His gut response surprised him, and he swiped a hand down his face, stubble scratching his palm. "No. She wouldn't want me anyway."

"I don't know about that. She was pretty worried about you last night. And fierce. Wouldn't let me help get you into bed. Said she wanted to check you for injuries."

His stomach clenched, and he glanced down. Still clothed, and to his relief, it felt like his leg was strapped on. At least she hadn't left him vulnerable in case Hunter walked in on him.

"I need to get home. Go away." He shoved the covers back, swung his legs over the side of the bed, groaning at the aches that registered all over his body.

"Yeah, about that. You're gonna have to stay here."

"Why?"

"Your cabin isn't exactly livable right now."

"What happened to it?"

"You did."

He clutched his spinning head, rested his elbows on his thighs. "Would you stop talking in circles?"

Hunter scratched his chin. "Looks like you ran out of booze, got mad, trashed the place. What happened to make you so mad anyway?"

Bits and pieces of the night before clicked into focus. He'd run out of whiskey, trying to drown the sounds of Madison's cries and screams. Drove into town.

Something else flickered at the edge of his memory. Something he'd seen. Or someone. Digging in a trash can.

He shook his head and stood up, braced his hand against the wall. Shuffled into the bathroom and forced himself to look in the mirror. A black eye, split lip, bruised jaw. Cuts scissored across the knuckles of both hands, so at least he'd gotten a few punches in. He lifted the tattered T-shirt up to see more bruises covering his torso. No wonder his ribs hurt.

"There's stuff in there if you want to shower." Hunter's voice drifted through the door. "And I'll leave a T-shirt on the bed for you. Might be tight, but it's better than what you're wearing."

Nash pulled the remains of his shirt off and tossed them in the trash, then brushed his teeth. Every movement hurt some part of his body, and he wanted to soak in his Jacuzzi. He wouldn't run the risk of showering at

Hunter's. Brother or not, he still didn't want any of them to know about his leg.

He walked out of the bathroom, and Hunter glanced at his body.

"How are you still upright? That guy beat the shit out of you."

Nash picked up the T-shirt and gingerly put it on. "Thanks for the bed and shirt." He walked out of the bedroom and headed to the back door, which would put him just that much closer to the path to his cabin.

"Want a ride somewhere?"

"Nope. Later." Making sure the door didn't slam and explode his head, he shuffled home through the trees. He wished for his sunglasses, but settled for squinting against the midday sun the whole way home instead.

Reaching his cabin, he noticed his truck parked in front. One of his brothers must've driven it home for him. There were several bags of trash lined up on the front porch, and the front door stood ajar. He pushed it open and stepped inside, looked around. Broken furniture was stacked on one side of the living room, and Kelsey was sweeping up a pile of debris.

"What're you doing?"

She jumped, dropping the broom. Bending over to pick it up pulled the jeans snug around her bottom.

Hungover as he was, he could still appreciate the view.

"How're you feeling?" she asked, turning toward him. Her eyes scanned his face, then lingered on Hunter's too-tight T-shirt.

"You don't need to be here cleaning up," he groused, embarrassed and mortified to no end that she'd seen him at his worst.

A flash of something crossed her face, then was gone. "I figured you wouldn't want anyone else nosing around, and you wouldn't be up to it." She swept glass into the dustpan, then tossed it in the trash can. "Why don't you go take a shower and I'll get you some food."

He grimaced. "Nah."

"You need to eat something."

"Only thing that'll help is some greasy food."

"Well, duh. Just go take a shower. I can smell you all the way over here."

Heat rose up his neck. He'd been trying not to smell himself, but she had a point. Changing course, he headed to his bedroom and opened the door. The bed was made, pillows fluffed and ready. The mirror from the dresser was gone. He vaguely remembered hurling something at it. Limping into the bathroom, he stripped down, then hurried through the shower as fast as his body would let him.

While he dried off, the scent of bacon drifted to him. It'd been a while since anyone had cooked for him, and his chest tightened. Shame and guilt washed over him. Kelsey was here to help him, understanding his need for privacy. He shuffled out to the kitchen just as she set a plate on the counter. He pulled out the one remaining bar stool and sat down.

Eggs, greasy hash browns and bacon stared up at him. He waited a beat to make sure his stomach wouldn't revolt, then tucked into the food.

"How is it?" she asked.

"Good. Thanks for cooking. But where'd it come from? I know I didn't have all this."

"I stopped by the lodge and swiped it from Mrs. Green." She grinned, and he couldn't help but grin back at her. The older woman had always had a soft spot for him.

"I appreciate you doing this. But you really didn't need to clean up, too."

She twisted a towel in her hands. "Gave me something to do. Didn't figure we'd have therapy today. And Maddy's having so much fun at day care, I took her up there anyway."

He shrugged, then winced as pain radiated from his ribs. "You got that right."

She walked around the counter to stand beside him, then pulled his T-shirt up, slid a hand along his left side.

The feel of her hand on his bare skin made him jerk.

"I checked your ribs last night, didn't think you'd broken any. Do you want to go get x-rayed in case you have a fracture?"

"No," he said, more harshly than he'd meant to.

"If you're injur—"

"I said no. Your hand is cold." He glanced sideways at her. Fact was, he wanted her hands all over his body, and it scared the hell out of him.

"Oh, sorry." She backed up a step and hesitated, then walked around the counter to the sink. Turning on the water, she squirted dish soap.

"Leave those. I'll get 'em." *Just go. Now.*

"You sure you're okay? Your voice sounds odd."

He looked up from the plate to see her frowning. "Just want a nap."

"Fine. But call me if you're still hurting later. I can give you a massage, and that might help."

He scrunched his eyes closed as images flashed through his mind. Him naked, her rubbing him, all over. Then her naked, and him doing a lot more than massaging. Heat snaked up his neck and all his blood pooled south of his waistband. "I'll be fine."

Her footsteps echoed across the now almost-barren

room. He sneaked a look around and saw her hesitate again. "What about furniture? Need help picking some out?"

"I lived in a tent in the desert for months at a time. This is luxury compared to that."

"Oh. Right. Well, see you tomorrow, if you're up for it." Her voice sounded funny.

He turned around on the stool. "Kelsey?"

She paused, one hand on the doorknob. "Yes?"

"Thanks," he said, his voice rough.

"You're welcome." She went out the door, closing it softly behind her.

And taking the sunshine with her.

Chapter Six

Kelsey spent the rest of the day paying the bills that had piled up while they were driving cross-country. At least now she had some funds to pay a few of them. Chewing her lip as she balanced her checkbook, her heart sank. The money sure had gone out the door fast.

A knock sounded at the door, and her mother walked into the room. "I'll get it, sweetie."

Looking up to see who was at the door, Kelsey saw a deliveryman holding a huge vase of flowers.

Her mother squealed. "Flowers! I just love flowers. Thank you so much, young man." She took the vase from him and closed the door. "I'll bet they're from Angus. Isn't he just the sweetest?"

The urge to warn her mother again about forming a relationship with her employer died on her lips as Bunny looked at the little envelope on the arrangement and frowned.

"These aren't for me. They're for you. Who on earth would be sending *you* flowers? And here, of all places?" She brought the vase to the desk and set them down, handed Kelsey the card.

"There must be some mistake." She read the outside of the envelope. It was her name all right. She slid a finger under the flap and opened it.

Thanks for last night. And for today. I appreciate it more than you know. Nash.

"Well? Who's it from?" Her mother still stood next to her, tapping her foot.

"It's nothing."

"Then why are your cheeks red?" Bunny grabbed the card and read it aloud, then smiled. "Is that where you went last night? And just what is he thanking you for?"

"Mom, he's my patient. I can't talk about him."

"I don't think he was a patient last night when you left here so late. Are you seeing him?"

"No, Mom. In fact, his brothers were there. He just got in a little trouble, and we helped him."

"I'll bet he didn't order flowers and have them rushed over for his brothers." Bunny cupped Kelsey's chin. "Angus told me Nash has been in trouble before. He used to get in fights, has always had an anger problem, and it's escalated since he got out of the Army."

Kelsey leaned back in the chair and crossed her arms. "Wouldn't you be angry if you lost—had been through as much as he was in the war? He's my patient. I have a professional relationship with him. That's it. I don't think you should be talking about him with Angus."

"I don't want to see you get hurt, that's all."

"I'm not going to. This is my job, you know. I've never gotten involved with patients before."

"I know. But you've also never worked with a really good-looking cowboy before. I mean, have you seen what those worn-out jeans do for his butt?"

"Mother! I can't believe you said that!"

Bunny laughed. "I may be old, but I'm still a woman. I'm telling you, you should check it out." She walked out of the room, giggling.

Kelsey shook her head, then leaned forward and sniffed the bouquet, losing herself in the scent. The arrangement was stunning, with hot pink roses and white hydrangeas. She'd seen a lot more than his butt the day before, and had wanted so badly to stare, drink him all in. Since Rob had died, she'd pretty much lived like a nun— no dates, no kissing, no nothing. They'd had a good sex life, and she missed the intimacy of being with a man. *With Rob. You've missed being with Rob.*

The night before, all she'd wanted to do was take care of Nash. It was obvious something had set him off, and he was hurting. Emotionally.

But it wasn't Rob she'd dreamed of when she finally got home at 4:00 a.m. Nash had filled her, time and time again, and she'd woken up aching that morning, wanting nothing more than to roll over and feel him next to her. On her. In her.

She'd debated about going to his cabin that morning, but figured he'd be sleeping all day, recovering at Hunter's. Having him walk in, wearing the tight T-shirt that contoured his muscles, had made her knees weak and her mouth water. Thank goodness he'd gone to take a shower. Cooking helped calm her down, but then he'd walked in again, and she'd wanted to jump him.

He's a patient. That's all he is and ever will be, she admonished herself.

Now if she could only take her own advice.

Common courtesy dictated she needed to thank him for the flowers, but with her emotions churning as they were, she didn't want to hear his voice. Couldn't hear his voice. So she sent him a text. And told him to let her know when he was ready to resume physical therapy, hoping she'd have at least a day to get over these feelings. Or at least find a way to hide them better. Hunter and her mother were far too perceptive. It would be catastrophic if Nash knew she was daydreaming about him.

A WEEK LATER, Nash pulled up to the corral at the main house in time to see Luke leading a black stallion down the ramp of the horse trailer. Sunlight gleamed off his shiny coat, and Nash itched to get his hands on that handsome beast. Cursing his bad leg once again, he resigned himself to the fact that he'd just have to watch his brother train a horse he secretly coveted.

"Hey, what took you so long in Vegas? Was the auction delayed?" Nash asked as he walked up to join Luke at the trailer.

"Nah. Did the auction, then stayed to play."

"Yeah? What's her name?"

"Who?"

"Whoever you liked enough to stay in Sin City with. You hate Vegas."

"When are you taking over the horses so I don't have to do that again?" Luke asked. The horse reared up, his front legs kicking. He fought to hold on to the reins and finally got the horse under a semblance of control. "You need to do your horse whisperer mojo thing with this one, Nash."

He shook his head slowly. "I'm kinda rusty. I'll just watch for now." He forced himself to back away and lean up against the fence post.

Luke led the horse into the corral and slipped the reins off, letting the horse go.

First thing Nash would have done, too. Let the horse get rid of all his anxiety about being cooped up in the trailer all the way from Vegas.

"What'd you name him?" he asked, keeping his eyes on the horse running around the corral.

"Midnight. I'm gonna grab a bottle of water out of the barn. You want one?"

Nash shook his head, intent on reading the horse. Trainers could tell a lot about a horse in the first run around a corral. He'd always ridden bulls in competition, but horses were his first love. And he was dying to get back to working with them. Not being cooped up like an invalid doing therapy every day.

A squeal of laughter caught his attention, and he squinted, looking for the noise. Kelsey's little girl was running around the yard. He looked around for Kelsey, but didn't see her or any other adult. He started heading her way, but hesitated, worried he'd scare her again.

It looked like she was chasing a butterfly as it flew through the air. Madison was laughing, not paying any attention to where she was going. And she was getting way too close to the corral where Midnight still ran loose. The butterfly flew into the corral, and Madison dropped down to crawl under the fence post and inside the ring.

His heart jackhammered in his chest.

It'd take too long to go around the outside to get to Madison. He opened the gate and ducked inside, hoping the horse would stay on the other side. But his plea went unanswered, and Midnight headed at a full gallop right toward the little girl.

Nash sped up, ignoring the sharp pain burning through his injured thigh. Reaching the little girl, he snatched her up even as he heard Midnight thundering behind him.

He curled her into his chest to protect her just as Kelsey reached him on the other side of the fence. He tossed Madison over the top post at Kelsey and started to drop down to roll under the bottom rung. But Midnight shoved him up against the fence. He shut his eyes, his body screaming as loud as the little girl was. "Get her out of here," he hollered as loud as he could, not wanting Madison to witness what a wild horse could do to a man.

Make it quick. Just get it over with.

Suddenly, the massive body holding him against the fence moved away. His fingers still clenched the wood, and he couldn't move them to let go.

"Nash."

A woman's voice sounded from far away, and he felt a hand on his fingers, trying to pry them away from the wooden fence. "Come on, Nash. I need to see how badly you're injured."

This time he recognized Kelsey's voice.

"Is your daughter hurt? I tried to get…"

"She's okay, just shaken up."

"Good. Glad she's okay…" His words slurred, and he started to slide down. His leg felt odd, as if the knee was out of joint. He tried to slide his bad leg underneath him for balance, then realized the prosthesis wasn't secured tight. One move and everyone would know.

"How bad is it?" Angus's voice boomed over his head, and Nash tried to see him.

"Call an ambulance," Kelsey said to his dad.

"No, don't…"

Angus pulled his phone out and flipped it open.

"Dad, no. I don't need an ambulance. I just need a minute."

"Son, a stallion pinned you to the fence. You need to get checked out."

Panic clawed its way up his throat. "I *need* you all to leave me the hell alone."

"Then what can I do?"

"Leave," Nash growled, opening his eyes to see Kelsey staring at him, Madison tucked tight against her body.

"Everyone just go. I'm fine, just had the breath knocked out of me."

"Fine." Angus stomped off, slamming the corral gate behind him.

"You okay, bro?" Luke asked.

"Yeah. What about the horse?"

"God, I'm sorry he went crazy on you. You sure you don't want to go get checked out?" He rubbed a hand across his chin. "You want me to get rid of him?"

"Not Midnight's fault. I know better. Had to get to Madison."

"How about I drive you back to the cabin? Need an ice pack or anything?"

Why was everyone treating him like a kid? "No. Just go away."

"Kelsey, why don't you bring Maddy up to the house?" Luke asked.

"Okay, thanks," she said.

Nash glanced at her out of the corner of his eye. He shook his head, just a tiny movement, hoping she'd understand.

"I'll be back, Nash," she said.

He looked over at Luke, who stared at him a beat longer, then turned on his heel and led the way to the big house.

Nash continued holding on to the fence, scared to let go. He hated to be so vulnerable. The seconds ticked by on the clock in his head, and he closed his eyes, focused on the sounds around him. An eagle screamed high above the field as it searched for a meal. Horses whinnied and nickered in the field behind him. A car backfired somewhere on the ranch, the sound echoing on the breeze. Guests splashed in the pool, their laughter drifting to him.

Normal, everyday sounds of life on a guest ranch.

But his life wasn't normal anymore. Would never be normal again.

Soft footsteps came down the path, and Kelsey's perfume reached him.

"Is Maddy okay?" he asked, opening his eyes as she walked inside the paddock.

She nodded. "She's fine. She's with my mom and your dad, holding court."

"Good," he muttered, relieved. "Anyone else hangin' around out here?"

Kelsey scanned the area, then met his gaze again. "No. So what's really wrong?"

"I think the binding on my leg busted. If I move, it'll come off."

"Oh."

"Can you help me to the toolshed?"

"Sure. Come on," she said, and scooted in close to him, wrapped her arm around his back.

He tried not to lean on her, but he had to shuffle and hold on to his leg. *Don't let it fall off out here. Last thing I need.* Every step felt like a burning hot poker shoving up through his thigh.

"Okay, hang on, and I'll get the door." She scooted out from under his arm to open the door, then came right back to him.

They shuffled inside the toolshed, and he pointed at the stool by the worktable against the far wall. Finally, he could sit down. The bindings chafed his leg, and he was pretty sure some had ripped apart.

Kelsey stood back, hands on hips. "Okay, what do you need?"

"Thanks. I'll take it from here."

"Nash, let me help."

"No," he growled. "Just leave me alone." He bent over,

rubbed the back of his neck, hoping she'd hurry up and leave.

"That won't work with me, you know."

He turned his head enough to squint up at her. "What won't?"

"Growling at me, pushing me away."

"I'm not doing that."

"Yes. You are. You're grousing at your brothers, your dad…it won't work with me. I'm in this for the long haul, so you might as well get used to it."

There went her spunk again. *I hate spunk*, he thought, even as he admired her for it.

"Just need to get this rewrapped and I can get out of here. Go on and take Maddy home."

He saw her pink tennis shoes, covered in dust and hay, move closer, into his line of sight. Jeans so old they had worn patches of white covered her legs, and he scanned up to her narrow waist. The short-sleeved blue T-shirt had seen better days, too.

He sat up slowly, which raised him to eye level with her breasts. On the small side, he thought and couldn't help but wonder what they looked like. Tipped in pink?

She folded her arms across her chest, and he jerked his eyes up to see her frowning. Her mouth was kicked up to the side, and that little freckle on her upper lip drove him crazy.

"What are you doing?"

"Just trying to figure out how a little thing like you can be so damn stubborn, obstinate and bossy."

"I took a class in med school."

He chuckled, and the smile crossing her face lit her up.

"Come on. Let's get you taken care of. I do need to take Maddy home."

Nodding, he reached down to pull the leg of his jeans

up. The thick fabric bunched, and he couldn't get it up all the way.

"Just take your jeans off. It'd be easier to fix the binding, wouldn't it?"

"I'd rather not strip down in front of you."

"Oh, get over yourself. I'm a medical professional."

Black dots danced in front of his eyes, and the back of his head tingled. "I'm just a missing leg to you, aren't I? One more job. Well I have news for you, Miss Medical Professional. I'm a man, dammit, and I barely have a shred of pride left."

Just get this over with. He fumbled for the button on his jeans, and he stood up enough to unzip them. Balancing on one leg, he started pushing them down, then overbalanced and started pitching forward.

Kelsey rushed in front of him, but his momentum was too much, and he fell forward, pinning her against the worktable. The binding shifted again, and he felt the prosthesis sliding. He froze, trying to stay upright.

Shock and pain ate at him, and rage that he'd ended up this way.

Gradually, he became aware that Kelsey was rubbing her hands up and down his back. The movements soothed him, and the red haze clouding his vision slowly receded.

She was a little thing, but it sure felt good to be pressed against her body. He breathed in, and the scent of some kind of flower drifted to him, just barely noticeable over the smell of saddle soap, oil and grease.

He leaned his head back a little to look down at her. Her lower lip was caught between her teeth, and her eyes were wide, staring up at him. Sliding his hands down her body, he cupped her butt and lifted her up onto the table.

Pure instinct drove him now, and he kissed her. Her lips were soft, and she tasted fresh and clean. He dived deeper, and she whimpered, her mouth opening to let his tongue in.

He felt her grip his shirt and she shifted, wrapping her legs around his hips.

"Kelsey," he rasped, sliding his mouth across her jaw, down her neck. Heat seeped through her jeans, and with his briefs the only barrier, his body hardened.

She was holding on to him now, so he wrapped an arm around her waist to hold her still and slid his hand beneath her T-shirt. Her skin was smooth and satiny, warm, and he wanted to touch her for days.

Drowning in the sensation of this woman, the sound of a shout outside the shed barely penetrated the fog in his brain.

Kelsey wrenched her mouth away from his, her breath coming in gasps. "Nash, stop. Let me go."

His own breath heaved, and he pulled back. She scooted out from between him and the table.

"That shouldn't have happened."

He hung his head, willed his body to cool down. It didn't work. If he'd had two good legs, he'd already be buried so deep inside her… Instead, the first woman he actually felt something for was telling him she didn't want him.

"Come on, let's get your—"

"Get out."

"It'll only take a sec—"

"I mean it. Get out now," he growled. "I don't want you here anymore. I don't need you."

"Nash…"

"You're fired."

Chapter Seven

Kelsey slammed the toolshed door behind her and stalked up the sidewalk toward the main house. She needed to calm down, so she tried some deep breathing and paced in a circle, kicking up dust. Nash's words echoed in her head, but the feel of his mouth on hers, his hands on her body, wouldn't let her calm down. Scrubbing a hand over her mouth to rid herself of his taste didn't help, either.

She wanted to go back in there and finish what he'd started.

Why hadn't she realized her body was so starved for a man's touch that she'd be turned on by that cranky, grouchy, stubborn, gorgeous hunk of man?

That's all it was. She hadn't been with anyone since Rob died almost three years ago. Normal, physiological, biological needs. That's all it was.

If that's all it was to her, she would've slept with someone since then. But she'd never been one to sleep around with just anyone. Rob had been her first—and her last. A stab of guilt pierced her heart, and her throat tightened.

She stopped pacing and stared up at the blue sky. Her body still ached where Nash had touched her, her lips still tingled. Clutching two fistfuls of hair, she yanked, hoping to dispel Nash's face looking at her with so much raw sexual desire.

She shook her head and tried to picture Rob, but his face was blurred around the edges.

"Hey, Kelsey."

She jumped, pressing a hand to her stomach when she saw Hunter in front of her. "Hey."

"You okay?"

"Yes."

"You don't look it." He frowned. "My big brother being a di— Er…a pain in the rump again?"

She relaxed a little. "You could say that. He just fired me. I really need this job."

Hunter rubbed a hand across his jaw. "Well, seein' how it was my dad who hired you, I don't think he can do that."

She thought about it a minute, then grinned. "I guess you're right."

"Come on up to Dad's house, and we'll get some lunch."

She looked at her watch. "I need to get Madison home."

"You both gotta eat, so come on up. There's always plenty of food." He slung an arm around her shoulder and steered her up the path.

A loud bang had her glancing over her shoulder, and she saw Nash standing in front of the shed, staring at her. He limped over to his truck, grabbed his Stetson off the hood, then climbed in. The truck roared to life, and he backed up, then sped down the driveway.

Guilt pricked at her. She should have stayed and helped him.

They reached Angus's house and went inside to the kitchen. She still marveled at how big it was, with all the most up-to-date stainless steel appliances. The exposed wood beams and log walls made the kitchen seem much cozier.

Angus sat by the fireplace, holding Maddy on his lap. He and her mother were talking to her daughter, who was laughing. When Maddy saw her, she scooted off his lap and hurled into her arms. "Mommy!"

She gathered her baby girl up and held her tight, shaking as she recalled how close she'd come to being trampled.

Angus stood up. "Is Nash okay? Does he need to go to the hospital?"

"No, he's fine," she said, keeping her face buried in Maddy's hug. She was torn, wanting to fill him in on Nash's condition, but still needing to respect her patient's wishes. It wasn't right of him to keep this huge thing from his family. *But, not my place to judge.*

Angus soothed a big hand over Maddy's back. "Madison has been telling me that Nash scared her today, and the other day, too. He shook his leg at her. Did he kick at her?"

Oh no. How do I answer this? "That's not what happened, sir. Maddy had run off from our picnic the other day and came across Nash at a pond." She covered Maddy's ears as best she could. "He was swimming and didn't have any trunks with him. Had to scramble to cover up," she whispered. *Please buy it.*

"She didn't see anything—" Concern etched his features, and she relaxed. That he cared enough to ask made her like him all the more.

"Oh no. It's okay. I'm going to take her home now and explain things. She has a tendency to run after butterflies."

"It can be dangerous on a ranch with trucks, horses and wildlife all over the place."

"Yes, sir. Thank you for watching after her. Hunter, thanks for the lunch invitation, but we need to get going." She turned to her mom. "You coming home, Mom?"

Bunny looked at Angus and blushed. "Angus has invited me to lunch and then a movie in town later on. I'll see you at home tonight, sweetie."

"Okay, see you later. Have fun, you two."

She glanced at Angus, surprised to see an almost-smitten look on his face as he gazed at her mother. Would wonders never cease? Her mom looked much the same. Hunter caught her eye and winked.

Picking up Maddy's bag, she packed them into the car and drove toward the cabin. Once there, she settled Maddy on the sofa.

"Sweetheart, we need to talk about something, okay? Put your baby down for a minute."

Madison set her doll down next to her and folded her hands in her lap.

"The other day when you saw Mr. Nash at the pond, you got really scared, right?"

Tears gathered in Maddy's eyes, and her lower lip trembled. She nodded.

"Well, Mr. Nash was hurt trying to protect some people, so Mommy is here to help him get better."

"Is he sick?"

"Well, no, not exactly. Some bad people hurt him, and now he doesn't have a leg anymore. He has one made of metal to help him walk. That's what you saw him holding the other day."

Maddy cocked her head and looked at her, a puzzled expression on her face. "What's metal?"

Kelsey looked around the room and saw the poker by the fireplace. She stood and reached for it, then sat back down. "This is metal. Feel how hard it is?"

Maddy reached out and gently poked at it. "Uh-huh. This is what he has now instead of a leg like mine?"

"It's just made like this, but it looks a bit different for him. Mr. Nash doesn't want anyone to know he has to use a metal leg now, so it's a big secret. Do you remember what a secret is?"

Maddy nodded, her face very serious. "It's like when Grandma kissed Mr. Angus and told me it's a secret."

Kelsey's eyes widened, and she fought not to laugh. "Yes, I guess that would be a secret, too. Just don't tell her you told me, okay?"

"Does Mr. Nash hurt when he walks?"

Her daughter had it right on the nose. "Yes, his leg really hurts him, so I'm trying to help him. But he hurts inside, too. He's a hero, and tried to protect lots of people, but he doesn't see it that way. And today, when you ran into the corral and that big horse was in there, he tried to protect you."

"He's not mad at me?"

"No, sweetie. He was scared that you would be hurt by the horse. That's why he ran so fast to you."

Madison looked down at her fingers. "So he was a hee-row today, too, right?"

"He sure was." Stroking a hand down Maddy's black hair, she ran her fingers through the tangles. She could never repay him for saving her little girl, but she'd find a way to try.

"I hope he feels good soon. I don't want him to be hurted."

"I know you don't. And I don't, either. So will you help me?"

Maddy nodded. "I want to help, too, Mommy."

"Okay, good. And remember, it's a secret. You can't tell anyone, even Grandma. Remember?"

"I won't tell."

"And as for you, you can't go running off anymore, okay? There's too many bad things that can happen to you. I know you love butterflies, but you have to stop chasing them. There are some big animals out here, and cars and trucks, and they may not see you in time to stop. Promise?"

"Okay, Mommy." Maddy yawned and picked up her doll. "Baby needs to go to sleep now. She wants me to lay down with her."

"That's a good idea. You carry your baby, and I'll carry mine." She picked Maddy up and took her to the bedroom. She snuggled her tight, then laid her down. "Love you, sweetie."

"Love you, Mommy. And Baby does, too."

Kelsey watched her, thankful Maddy was fine.

Now if only she could figure out what to do about her grouchy patient.

Without losing her heart in the process.

NASH'S PHONE DINGED the next morning, and woke him up. He fumbled for it on the nightstand, and read a text from Kelsey.

Rise & shine, Cowboy. Therapy starts in 30. Meet me on porch.

He grimaced, then texted back. I fired you.

His phone dinged again.

You can't. Get moving.

He shook his head. Hell I can't. You're still fired.

Ding. Another text from Kelsey. *Only Angus can fire me. 25 min.*

What the hell was she up to? He shoved the covers off and reached for his leg, every movement hurting. His fault for getting in the way of a nervous horse. He strapped the leg on, still wanted to hurl it across the room, but at least he was resting his leg every night. Pulling on clothes and boots, he wondered why she hadn't quit when he gave her the chance.

Thirty minutes later, he opened his front door, surprised to see Kelsey sitting on Bubba, one of the horses their more advanced guests used. She held the reins to his own gelding. "What're you doing?"

"I'm going riding. What does it look like I'm doing?"

"I fired you. Can't you ever do what you're told?"

"Since your dad hired me, only he can fire me." She grinned, and damned if he didn't want to laugh.

Scowling instead, he stroked a hand down Thunder's nose. "You said I wasn't ready to ride." Remembering their kisses from the day before, he added, "Horses, that is."

A blush of pink colored her cheeks. "There will be no more of that. I'm a professional. That's why I'm here. Not to let you compromise me."

He raised an eyebrow. "Compromise? What is this, Victorian London?"

The blush on her cheeks deepened. "I fell asleep reading a historical romance last night. But you know what I mean. We need to keep this professional. Got it?"

"Got it." He reached inside the door and grabbed his Stetson, clapped it on his head, anxious to see if he could do this. He shut the door, then limped to the steps, but hesitated.

"You probably don't want to hear my advice, much

less do it, but I think if you mount from the step, it'll be easier this first time." She guided her horse next to Thunder's side and handed him the reins.

Guiding his left leg into the stirrup, he grabbed the pommel and slung his right leg over the saddle. The horse shifted, and a small tremor ran through Nash. Sweat broke out on his brow. What if he wasn't ready for this? What if he would never be ready for this? All he wanted to do was get back on a horse and prove he could still do his job on their ranch.

"How's that feel?"

"Fine," he snapped.

Without another word, Kelsey clicked to her horse, and they turned toward the path leading to the trailhead.

Guilt pricked his gut. She was only trying to help. No need to snap at her for helping him do the very thing he'd wanted to do all along. Ride again.

He clicked to get Thunder moving, and they set off after her. Keeping his legs as still as possible, he kept Thunder to a walk. At least till he got his sea legs back, so to speak.

The morning air was crisp and cold, with a hint of wood smoke drifting to him. The sun rose a little higher, just peeking over the mountain ridge, turning the morning pink and orange.

Kelsey glanced back once at him, and he tipped his hat to her. In apology, more than anything. The steady pace soothed him, even as he itched to give Thunder the signal to break into a full gallop. But she'd probably just yell at him again.

She kept her own horse to a walk in front of him. He noticed she really did seem at home on a horse. Her back was straight, and she sat tall in the saddle, even if she was just a little bitty thing. He wondered where she'd gotten the cowboy hat. It looked old and worn, as did the matching brown boots. The puffy vest she had on covered up her curves, so he had to imagine them. Then his thoughts got the better of him, and he pictured her wearing just the vest, and nothing else. He'd unsnap it slowly, slide a finger along her chest, then her stomach, as her skin was revealed.

His horse whinnied, and he jerked out of the daydream of a naked Kelsey. She'd dismounted and waited for him, reins looped around the fence post of the old hunting shack. They'd gone a lot farther than he'd figured if they'd reached this old place. No wonder his thigh ached.

It pissed him off to have to use the steps like a kid, but he didn't want to set his recuperation back any further by being stubborn. He lined the horse up parallel to the steps and climbed off. His leg wobbled when he put weight on it, but at least he remained upright. This time.

"How do you feel?"

He kept his back to her so she wouldn't see the eye roll. Yes, she was asking as a therapist. But would she ever see him as a man? A man who wanted her? He stopped, shocked to realize he really did want her.

"Nash?"

"Yeah?"

"How's your leg? Do you need to rest—"

"Nope," he answered over his shoulder. "Doing good. Thanks for getting me back on a horse." He turned his head just enough to see her out of the corner of his eye. Didn't she know when she frowned her little freckle drove him nuts?

"Want some coffee?"

"You brought some?"

She unbuckled the saddlebag, pulled out a thermos and set it on the porch. "Figured you might not have had any." She walked around the other side of the horse and fiddled with something, then came back holding a container. "Muffins, too."

His stomach growled, and she laughed.

"Guess you're hungry, too. Do you want to go inside or eat out here?"

He pointed to the table and chairs sitting in the corner of the porch. "Why, al fresco, of course." He grabbed a chair and turned it upright.

Her eyebrows popped up.

"What, you still think I'm just a hick cowboy from Montana?" He grinned, then turned over another chair.

A smile spread over her face, and she shook her head. "Nope. I've found you have a few undiscovered depths. I shouldn't be amazed anymore by you."

A little bubble of happiness burst in his chest, taking him completely by surprise. He found he wanted to put more smiles on her face.

A little shaken, he gestured to her chair, and they ate in companionable silence, the day coming alive around them.

"It really is beautiful out here," she said, breaking the quiet.

"You sound surprised."

"I am. I grew up in Florida. I wasn't too sure what to expect when we came here." As she spoke, she unsnapped the puffy vest and shrugged out of it.

Not quite what he'd hoped for, but the Western shirt suited her, hugging her figure. She stood, took her hat off and hung it on a hook on the wall. As she stretched, her shirt pulled tight across her chest.

He reached out and grabbed her, pulling her onto his lap.

Her deep blue eyes were big and wide as she stared at him. "Don't—"

He pressed a finger against her lips to halt the flow of words he knew would follow. "I'm a healthy male—well, relatively speaking—and you're a very desirable woman." He traced a finger over her lips. "I haven't wanted anyone in a long time, especially not since I woke up in a hospital in Germany."

"No one?" she asked, her voice very quiet.

"No one. Sure, a few of the nurses flirted with me, but I knew they just felt sorry for me."

"You don't know that."

"Well, I didn't want any of them. None of them interested me like you do." Keeping his eyes on hers, he slowly reached up and took his own hat off, set it on the table. He tilted her head a bit to the side and kissed the very freckle that had driven him crazy. "I've wanted to do that since I met you."

"You didn't like me very much when we first met."

He shrugged. "Doesn't matter. I still wanted to."

Her breath hitched, and he felt it all the way to his groin. "Shh. It's okay. I won't hurt you."

He knew this probably wasn't a good idea, but he had to taste her again. Leaning forward, he kissed her lips, gently, until she opened her mouth. He swept in, groaning when her tongue met his, tangling, taunting, turning him on even more than he was.

Suddenly she pushed against his chest. "Let me up."

Rejection stung, sharp and hot.

Chapter Eight

Kelsey watched his eyes go flat as she stood up, his expression closing her out. She faced him, then put her hands on his legs and pushed them closer together. Straddling his legs, she sat back on his lap, facing him, getting as close as she could to him.

His body jerked, and the look on his face almost broke her heart.

After tossing and turning all night, she still hadn't known what she should do if he made a pass at her again. But her body cried out for him now. Ached, in fact.

Sure, he could be surly and angry, but he also cared about her daughter, which was a huge plus in her book.

And he made her feel things in places she thought had died along with Rob.

His arms came around her, pressed her close. He buried his face in her neck, and his shoulders relaxed as she held him.

"I didn't think to ask if you have someone in your life." His words were muffled against her neck.

This was it, her way out. "No. But I haven't done this in a long time."

He pulled back and smoothed a strand of hair off her cheek. "Done what? Kissing?" He grinned.

Heat crept up her cheeks, and she squirmed, but froze when she felt his hard ridge nudge her. "Anything."

The grin faded from his face. "At all?"

She nodded, looking anywhere but at his face.

He cupped her head, forcing her to look at him. "No one, since…"

"Rob died."

"That long?"

She'd expected derision, not shock, from him. "I haven't wanted to be with anyone."

"Haven't you dated?"

"No time. Taking care of my daughter is my priority, and I've been trying to pay—" She clamped her lips shut.

"Pay what?"

She shook her head.

"Babe, you can tell me anything."

Shutting her eyes, she blurted out, "Pay off the debts my husband left."

Dead silence.

She cracked an eyelid open.

Nash was frowning. "I didn't know. I'm sorry."

She shrugged. "That's what happens when you invest in risky ventures. So there just hasn't been any time for—" She waved a hand between them. "Anything like this. No one's interested me, either."

There. She'd said it. Now he'd think she was as frozen and frigid as she'd felt the last couple of years.

His eyes squinted, and she could almost see the steam coming from his ears. "So this—" he mimicked her hand gesture, waving it between them "—is pity for the crippled guy?"

Anger spiked, hot and heavy in her gut. She pushed away from him and stood up, paced away from him, then back. "No, you ding-dong dumbass. You're the first one

I've felt anything for. I can't sleep, because every time I close my eyes, I see you there."

She couldn't read the look on his face, but he grabbed her, pulled her back to straddle his legs. He crushed his mouth to hers, and it felt so good she almost swooned. His lips devoured hers, took everything she had, then gave it all back to her.

He shifted, rolling his hips, and his hardness pressed against her again. *Right there.* She whimpered, and he slid his hand around to cup her breast. Heat pooled low in her belly.

"I need more," he groaned against her mouth, then sat back and unsnapped her shirt. He groaned again when her white lacy bra was revealed, and he traced the outer edge, just where her breast swelled.

Both of the horses whinnied and shook their harnesses. Movement in one of the trees behind Nash's head caught her eye, and she squinted in the bright light. Her blood ran cold, and she froze.

"Nash, stop."

"Can't."

She pushed at him. "There's a bear," she hissed, afraid to speak too loud.

He went still as a statue. "Where?"

"Behind you, in the trees about twenty yards away."

He slowly turned his head. "It's up in one of the trees, eating."

She stared at the bear, who was indeed now in a spindly looking tree. It scooped branches and leaves toward its snout.

"Don't make any sudden movements." He slowly set her off his lap and stood, watching the bear the whole time. "We need to walk the horses in the opposite direction, but go slow."

They picked up the remains of their breakfast, but her heart was pounding so hard she almost couldn't breathe.

He glanced at her, one side of his mouth kicking up, then reached for her and snapped the shirt closed again. "I hate doing that. Sure looked pretty."

Heat suffused her cheeks, and she couldn't believe she'd forgotten about being exposed to him. Much less to a bear.

"Um, Nash? Bear?"

"Just keep moving slow. No sudden movements. Don't want to attract any attention," he said, his voice low.

She followed his lead, praying they'd make it to safety before the bear noticed them. They got their horses and started walking back the way they came. Peeking behind her once more, she whispered, "Why isn't he paying attention to us?"

"Having his own breakfast."

"But in a tree?"

"Berries."

"I'd heard bears can climb trees, but I've never seen one do it." Another glance behind her, and she breathed a sigh when she could barely see it any longer. "Heck, I've never seen a bear outside a zoo before."

"Welcome to Montana." He looked behind them and stopped his horse. "I think we can ride now. We're far enough away."

She started to mount her horse, then realized there was no step for Nash to use. Peeking over the horse's back, she saw him standing next to his own mount, head leaning against its powerful shoulder. The back of his neck was red, and she waited for the backlash.

The minutes ticked by, and he still hadn't moved or spoken. She debated about saying anything but didn't want to upset him.

"I grew up on a horse," he said, still not looking at her. "That I can't get back up on my own is the hardest part. Makes me feel less of a man..." His words trailed off, but there was a world of pain in his voice, and she could only imagine what the words cost him in pride.

She walked around her horse to stand next to him. "You never have to worry about that."

He turned away from her, his shoulders hunched.

"Listen to me. You're the manliest man I've ever met. The outside package isn't what counts. It's what's inside, here." She rested her hand over his heart, wishing he would actually hear her, realize the truth in her words.

"We need to get moving. Clouds are rolling in. Get on your horse."

"You first."

HE FROZE, then turned his head, glaring at her, eyes narrowed.

"You've been working with weights, right? May just give you enough leverage to get up without a step or block."

He clenched his teeth against the torrent of curses building up in his head. She just stood there, watching him with those pretty eyes. If he tried this and failed... It'd be the worst kind of humiliation.

He guided his left foot into the stirrup, gripped the pommel and tried to heave himself up. His muscles shook, and he almost gave in, but felt her hands shove against his backside. The momentum got him going, and he made it up into the saddle.

Anger, bruised pride and relief all warred together, and he glanced down to see her grinning at him. "Did you have to do that?"

"It worked, didn't it? First time is always the hardest." She walked back around her horse and took the reins. "Besides, maybe I just wanted to get my hands on your ass."

He burst out laughing at her cheeky words. God, how he wanted this woman. She wasn't like anyone he'd ever known before. Checking his watch, he noted it was almost noon. Maybe he could convince her to go to his cabin, and they could continue where they left off on the porch.

With a whoop, she kicked her horse into a gallop, and he watched her, unable to stifle another laugh. Clicking to Thunder, he started at a trot and followed her.

Thirty minutes later, they neared her cabin and slowed. "I just want to make sure Mom and Maddy are okay, then we can go on to your cabin so I can check your leg."

His enjoyment dimmed a bit, but she was right. He hadn't ridden in years, and his thigh was aching. Then he glanced at her and saw her smile. Maybe he *could* talk her into—

A loud crash reverberated from the cabin, followed by a woman's scream. Kelsey scrambled off her horse. He hurried as fast as he could, but when his left leg touched the ground, he started to crumple. Catching hold of the pommel, he held still. Once he knew he wouldn't fall, he looped the reins for both horses around the fence post and limped toward the front porch, then inside the cabin.

Bunny Randolph lay on the floor, a broken chair next to her. Madison sat next to her, crying. Kelsey knelt next to her mother.

"What happened?"

All three women looked up at him. Bunny preened a little, then grimaced when she moved her arm. The little girl leaned away from him, then looked at her mother, and miracle of miracles, she stopped crying.

"I was on the chair trying to move some things around on the bookcase. I must have overbalanced and fallen off."

"I'm going to drive you into town, Mom. You need to get X-rays. I don't see any punctures, but it could be fractured. Hold still, and I'll make a splint." She stood up and hurried out of the room.

He felt helpless, so set to picking up the pieces of the chair.

"I'm so sorry I broke the chair, Nash. I'll reimburse you all for it."

"Don't worry about it. It's just some wood. I'm more worried about you." He knelt by her as best he could and peeked at Madison, who sat staring at his leg.

"Mom, hold still and I'll get this wrapped around your arm, then we can go."

"Can I do anything to help?"

Kelsey glanced up at him. "Could you grab my purse and the big bag next to it on the floor? Then maybe help my mother to the car while I get Maddy ready to go?"

"I'll stay here with Maddy." His eyes popped wide-open when he realized what he'd just said, and he glanced at Kelsey.

She hesitated and looked at her daughter. "That would be great, but are you sure? I don't know how long we'll be gone. What about the horses?"

"I'll get a couple of ranch hands out to get the horses and take care of them. And I can always call Mrs. Green to help if I need to." Sweat beaded on his forehead, and he wiped his sleeve across it. *What the hell am I getting myself into?*

Kelsey finished splinting her mom's arm, then took Maddy into the other room. Helping Bunny to the car, he winced every time she did. A fall at her age had to be serious. He got her settled in and gently buckled her seat belt.

"You're a good boy, Nash. Thank you." She patted his cheek, then leaned her head back against the seat.

A warm glow spread through him, and he went back inside the cabin. Kelsey and Maddy were just coming out of the bedroom, and the little girl clutched a doll in a death grip.

"You be my good girl, and mind Mr. Nash, okay? Remember what we talked about?" Kelsey asked, then kissed Maddy's cheek.

Maddy nodded, a solemn look on her face.

Kelsey kissed his cheek, then blushed a bright shade of pink. "Thank you, Nash. I really appreciate this."

"You go on and take your mom into town. We'll be fine."

Her expression changed to pensive, and he realized his words sounded a little strangled. "It's okay. Go on."

She hurried out the door and closed it, leaving him alone with the kid. Pulling out his cell phone, he called the stables and arranged for the horses to be picked up and taken care of. Then he looked at his watch just as his stomach growled. "Did you eat lunch yet, Maddy?"

She nodded, still not letting go of her doll.

"You mind if I get a snack? I'm hungrier than a bear..." He immediately thought of what he and Kelsey had been doing when she spotted that bear earlier in the day. Heat crept up his neck. Better get his mind off that track. "So will you show me where the kitchen is?"

She raised a tiny hand and pointed toward the kitchen. He knew where it was, but he was desperate to get her to talk.

"Well, thank you, ma'am," he drawled. Maybe he

could turn on some cowboy charm and get her to talking. "What do you think I should have for a snack?"

She just stared up at him.

Great.

"You want to go with me to the kitchen, show me
where your mom keeps the food?"

She stared up at him, then cocked her head. Reaching
up, she surprised the hell out of him by latching on to his
hand. She led him toward the kitchen, then dropped his
hand and pointed at the pantry.

"Thank you, Maddy." He hunted up bread and cheese,
and grilled up some cheese sandwiches. A beer sounded
really good right about now, but no way would he drink
on the job. He sat at the kitchen table and ate his lunch,
then made quick work of cleaning up the kitchen, all
while she stared at him.

He patted his stomach. "Well that was good. Thanks
for keeping me company while I ate. You want to go
watch some TV with me?"

Maddy turned and headed out the door, back to the
living room. He followed her, and saw her standing by
the couch with the remote in her hand. Sinking down
on the leather sofa, he took it from her. "What should
we watch?"

She shrugged, so he shrugged and clicked the TV
on, searching for something that wouldn't bore either of
them. He had no idea what kids watched. "You tell me
if you see something you want to watch, okay?" *Other
than me*, he thought when he saw her still staring at him.

Maddy leaned against the couch and looked up at the
TV. He settled on a Scooby-Doo cartoon, and at least
she was watching it.

Sharp pains shot through his thigh, and he rubbed it.
He shifted, trying to get more comfortable. Digging his

fingers into his leg, he tried to ease the aches. Out of the corner of his eye, he saw Maddy turn toward him, staring at his leg. Then she turned and fled the room.

He shut his eyes, a hard ball lodging in his throat. At this point, nothing would ever win her over. How could he try for anything with Kelsey when her daughter was terrified of him?

Something tapped his arm, and he opened his eyes to see Maddy standing in front of him. She glanced at his leg again. "Does your leg hurt?"

He nodded slowly, bracing himself for tears, or worse. "Yes, it does."

She opened a box and pulled something out, then held it out to him. He took it and looked at it.

A pink Band-Aid. With white daisies on it.

"This is what my mommy puts on me when I get a boo-boo."

His heart cracked, just a tiny bit, and he blinked his eyes. "Thank you, honey."

"Mommy said you got hurted being a hee-woh. You saved people from the bad men."

"She told you that, huh?" he whispered.

She nodded, a very serious look on her face, then tapped the Band-Aid. "That will make you all better."

He couldn't very well put it on his thigh without disrobing, which he would never do. No time like the present to see how she'd react to his leg now. He pulled the wrapper off the Band-Aid, braced his foot on the coffee table and pulled the leg of his jeans up just above his boot. The metal glinted in the light from the TV, and he looked at Maddy to see how she would react.

She studied the prosthesis, but didn't say anything.

"Do you want to touch it? It won't hurt you."

She looked up at him, then gingerly touched the metal.

Silently, she took the pink Band-Aid from him, peeled back the tabs and put it across the shin. Then she leaned over and kissed it. "Mommy always kisses my boo-boos. That makes it better, right?"

Nodding, he opened his arms wide, and she crawled onto his lap. That tiny fissure in his heart widened, and he fell hard for this little miniature of Kelsey.

Chapter Nine

Fighting exhaustion, Kelsey pulled up in front of the cabin and nudged her mother awake. Thank God it was only a sprain, but she would have to take it easy for a while. She got out of the car and helped her mother. They headed up the porch steps, and she fumbled to open the door.

The lights in the living room were on low, the television tuned to a cartoon. Maddy's old tea set was spread out on an overturned box, stuffed animals decorated the floor and Candy Land was scattered on the coffee table. Nash sat on the couch, head resting against a pillow, with Madison on his lap, an arm curled around her. She raised her head from Nash's chest to look at Kelsey, then put her finger to her lips.

A tiny giggle erupted from Bunny, and she hurried to her bedroom, holding her uninjured hand over her mouth.

Kelsey tiptoed to the couch and picked Maddy up off Nash's lap.

"Mommy, Mr. Nash needs sleep. He's weally tired."

"I see that, sweetie. You must be tired, too. Did you eat dinner?"

Maddy nodded. "Mr. Nash cookeded, and it was yummy."

"You ready for bed now?"

Maddy yawned and nodded her head.

Kelsey took her baby girl to the bedroom and got her changed into her favorite pink pajamas. She settled Maddy into bed, and by the time she'd walked to the door and peeked again, she was out.

She checked on her mother, who was also out like a light, then headed back to the living room. Grabbing the remote from the coffee table, she clicked the TV off and braced herself to look at Nash.

He'd wormed his way into her mind, then today, into her heart. Yes, he was grumpy and grouchy, and could even be surly, but after all he'd been through, she understood. He shifted and brought a hand up to scratch his chest. Something was on the back of his hand, and she looked closer.

One of Maddy's pink Band-Aids.

She clapped a hand over her mouth to stifle the laughter. Maddy only shared those with special people.

Nash's eyes opened, and he sat up abruptly. "Where is she?"

"I put her to bed. Tha—"

He grabbed her arm and pulled her down on his lap, then kissed her. Oh boy, did he kiss her. His lips should be registered as lethal weapons, because his kisses were doing something to her body, and she didn't want it to stop.

Threading his fingers through her hair, he eased back. "I was just dreaming about you. I opened my eyes, and there you were."

One finger traced her lips, and she glanced down at his large hand. She smiled and took his hand in her own, holding it up. "I can't believe Maddy gave you one of her special Band-Aids."

"She saw my busted-up knuckles from the other night.

Kissed it to make it better, too." He scooted her off his lap and onto the couch next to him, and she missed his warmth immediately. "But that's not all she did. She saw me rubbing my leg." He leaned forward and hitched his pant leg up. Five pink Band-Aids crisscrossed his prosthesis.

Tears filled her eyes, and she looked up to meet his gaze.

"She's one special little girl, Kelsey. You're lucky to have her."

"She's not scared anymore?"

He shook his head. "Guess not. Whatever you said to her made an impression." Clearing his throat, he took her hand in his, twined their fingers together. "Thanks for that, by the way."

"You're welcome." She squeezed his hand, and it felt odd to be held by a man's hand again. "It's true, you know. You are a hero."

His grip on her hand tightened. "No. I'm not." He stood up. "I need to get going. I'm sure you're exhausted."

Bewildered at his abrupt change of mood, she stood, put a hand on his arm. "You said your leg was hurting earlier. How's it doing now?"

"Fine."

Now she gripped his sleeve. "Nash. How is it really?"

He rolled his eyes. "It hurts, okay? I'm going to go soak in the Jacuzzi."

At least he could admit it now. "Want a massage?"

He shook his head. "You look beat. Go to bed."

"Thank you for staying. It really helped, especially since we had to wait so long at the ER."

"Your mom okay?"

"Just a sprain." She took his hand and led him to the

door. "I mean it. Thank you." Rising up on her tiptoes, she kissed his stubbled cheek.

"You're welcome. Night, Kelsey." And he left without another word or look back.

Now what did I do? She thought back over their conversation. He seemed to shut down when she said he was a hero. Was that it? Why did it bother him so much?

Smiling, she remembered how the pink bandage looked on his big, tanned hand. Her heart had turned over, and it scared her. While every day seemed like a lifetime without Rob, it had still been almost three years. Maybe she should go out on a date. Share some kisses with a very hot cowboy.

But that's all it could be.

She still needed to find a job, and more patients, so she could finish paying off the debts. It would be too hard to get involved with Nash and then have to move on.

Her phone dinged with a text message alert.

Dr. appt tmrw in Billings. Want to go?

Billings? Not sure of her geography, she flipped to the maps app on her phone and plugged in the city. A three-hour drive each way. That much time enclosed in a car with Nash? A part of her shivered with anticipation. Another in dread. But it would be a good chance for her to hear straight from the doctor how her patient was doing.

Need a sitter. Can I get back to you?

Chkd w/ Mrs. G. She's good to go.

He'd already checked? She sighed, pleased he'd thought of her daughter so quickly.

OK. Time?

Pick u up @ 6:30.

"Kelsey? Anything wrong?"

She turned at the sound of her mother's voice. "Nash just texted. He has a doctor's appointment tomorrow and asked me to go with him." Spying her mother's sling, she grimaced. "I better tell him I can't go. I don't want to leave you."

"Nonsense, pumpkin. Angus called a little while ago to check on me. He's going to take me up to the lodge tomorrow and keep an eye on me."

"Are you sure? I hate abandoning you."

"You're not abandoning me. You're giving me the chance to have a very handsome man fuss over me. Maddy can go to her day care, and then stay with me, so you don't have to worry about that. You go spend the day with *your* very handsome man."

Seemed to Kelsey her mother was doing some matchmaking of her own. "I keep telling you Nash is my patient. I just want to be there at the doctor's appointment to see what he has to say. Nash may not be as forthcoming telling the doc what he needs to if I'm not there."

Her mom winked at her. "You betcha. Now, you better get to bed and get your beauty sleep. We've had a long day and I know you're tired, too."

Kelsey helped her mom back to her bedroom and got her settled, then headed to her own room. She opened her closet door and peered at her meager clothes. She needed to be professional for the doctor's appointment, yet she still wanted to look pretty for—

What am I doing? This isn't a date! He's my patient. Just. A. Patient.

NASH IDLED HIS truck outside Kelsey's cabin and saw her walk out the door just as he was about to get out. She waved and hurried to the passenger side before he could open the door for her.

"Morning."

"Hey. You're chipper this morning."

She smiled and held up a travel mug. "I'm on my second cup of coffee, so that helps." Holding up a bag, she said, "I also packed us some cinnamon rolls, whenever you get hungry."

He took a deep breath, and the aroma of hot cinnamon mixed with her own fresh-from-the-shower scent. "Smells good enough to eat." And with his words, his mind immediately went to just what it was he wanted to eat.

"Nash?"

He took his mind out of the bedroom and looked at her.

"I asked why the appointment is in Billings and not in town."

"This doctor was recommended by the Army surgeon who worked on me. They went to med school together."

"I see."

True, the doctor in Billings had been recommended to him, but so had one locally. He just didn't want anyone so close to home knowing yet. Or ever.

THREE HOURS LATER, they pulled into the parking lot of a medical center. Luckily they didn't have long to wait. Once the doctor had given him a full examination, they had the nurse bring Kelsey back to talk to the doctor. Nash had already cleared it with the doctor and signed papers so she could be given information about his condition.

"Nash is doing well, but I'm concerned about the redness and bruising on his thigh. I've recommended he get an additional prosthesis. You all can go straight downstairs to be fitted for a new one." The doctor turned to Kelsey. "How's he doing with therapy?"

"I've devised a daily regimen, and he seems to be getting stronger already. We did have an incident with a horse a few days ago. It knocked him up against a fence post and pinned him."

Now why'd she have to go and say that?

The doctor turned to him. "Is that where the bruising came from?"

"Yes." He tried to school his features so he wouldn't throw the glare he wanted to at her.

"Anything else happen?"

He could just feel her stare burning a hole in his head, but he kept silent.

"The bruises from the horse were layered in over bruising from a fight."

This time he did turn his head and glare at her. She folded her arms and stuck her tongue out at him. It surprised him so much he almost laughed.

"Aren't you old enough to know fighting doesn't accomplish anything? Especially in your condition?"

He shrugged. "Fights happen."

The doctor glanced at Kelsey. "Sounds like this may go deeper than just a bad day. Have you thought about talking to a psychologist?"

"I don't need a shrink. It was just a bad day at the ranch."

"Then I suggest you don't end bad days in a bar." The doctor tore a sheet off a pad and handed it to him. "Make sure you have them take a look at your current prosthesis downstairs. I want to make sure nothing was bent from either incident."

Kelsey cleared her throat. "Doctor, I've done therapy using horses before, and I took Nash on a ride yesterday. I hope you're okay with that. He grew up on a horse, and I know he's been wanting to get back on one."

"I think a short ride once or twice a week is fine. Just don't overdo it."

The doctor shook hands with of them and led them to the door. "Make an appointment to come back in a month, or sooner if you feel anything is wrong."

Leaving the office, they waited for the elevator in silence. Once the doors opened, he let her go in first, then hit the button for the lower floor. "Did you really have to tell on me?"

"I know you're not happy about that, and I'm sorry. But as your therapist, I have to keep your doctor apprised of your health. It's for your own good." She put her hand on his arm. "Please understand that I want you to be healthy. And don't hate me too much, okay?"

He glanced down at her slim hand on his arm. No one outside his family had ever cared about him this much. Looking back up at her pretty face, his gaze lingered on her lips. "I don't hate you. And I know you care. That's what makes you a good therapist."

The elevator stopped, and they headed for the office the doctor had sent them to for the prosthesis. He opened the door and let her go in first, then followed. The waiting room was half-full, all amputees of one form or another. Dread filled him, and he started backing out the door. Kelsey grabbed his hand and pulled him inside.

Keeping his gaze straight ahead, he signed in, then sat down in the far corner next to Kelsey. If she hadn't been there, he'd have skipped this. A stack of newspapers sat next to him on a side table, and he grabbed one, opening it up so it covered his view of the room. None of the articles caught his attention until he saw one about a rodeo taking place in Billings. He checked the date of the newspaper. Today would be the second day of the rodeo, and bull riding was the main event.

He set the newspaper down. "Want to go to a rodeo today?"

She looked at him, frowning. "Today?"

"I just saw the ad in the paper. It's the second day, but we could still catch several events."

She glanced at her watch. "When would we get home?"

"Late tonight." He glanced at her. "We don't have to go if you'd rather get home."

"Okay. I guess we could go for a little while. I just want to make sure we're home before Maddy's bedtime."

"Sure, we can just go for a couple of hours. Thanks."

AN HOUR LATER they were on the way to the fairgrounds at the edge of town. He parked and they walked toward the entrance where the events would take place.

"I've never been to a rodeo before."

He glanced at her. "You haven't? Ever?"

She shook her head. "Not once."

"Then you're in for a great experience."

He bought their tickets and stopped to get popcorn and sodas, then led her to the stands. The smell of horses, hay and leather mingled with the fried food in the concession area. Lights gleamed overhead, spotlighting the cowboy hats bobbing around the pens. Metal clanged as a bull butted up against the pen. It all took him way back, and his gut clenched as he realized just how much he'd missed being a part of the rodeo scene.

They found seats near the side railing, a few rows up, parallel to the bull pens. It felt odd to be on this side of the stadium seating, instead of down below where the action happened.

Barrel racing was center ring, and he tried to pay attention, but his gaze kept getting pulled to the pens, and the line of cowboys leaning against the railing. He recognized a couple of men from his earlier years. One of the younger guys glanced at him, then did a double take. He whispered to another kid, and they all turned around to stare at him.

Maybe this wasn't such a good idea.

Chapter Ten

Kelsey tore her eyes from the barrel racer in the ring as someone climbed up the outside of the railing where they were sitting.

"Mr. Sullivan, right? Boy, howdy. This is great. We haven't seen you in years!" A man with bright red curls and freckles hung on to the railing, grinning for all he was worth.

Nash brushed her arm as he reached over to shake the young man's outstretched hand. "Hey, Jimmy. Been in the Army. Just got home a couple months ago."

"You wanna come over, see the bulls? Say hi to the guys?"

Nash rubbed the back of his neck. "I wouldn't want to get in the way. Besides, can't leave my date alone."

Date?

He glanced at her, almost as if he wanted her to speak up.

"Promise it won't take long. But Rodney over there is ridin' today, and I'll bet he could use some pointers from you."

Nash shifted, standing up to scan the bull pens. Then he glanced down at her. "You mind? Won't be gone long."

Something in his voice made her study him closer.

"Sure, go ahead." He had seemed almost wistful, and now he was vibrating with excitement. "I'll be here."

The kid whooped and hopped down the railing, then raced back to the pens. Nash followed, thank goodness using the steps, not the railing.

She watched him walk toward the other cowboys, and they swallowed him up, shaking his hand, clapping him on the back. Jimmy dragged him farther down the line, and all the men leaned up against the fence again. What a sight they made—a row of cowboy hats, dusty jeans and boots. She pulled her phone out of her bag and focused on the long row of cowboys, snapped a picture, then texted it to her mother.

Stopped at a rodeo. Figured you'd want to see this view.

Her phone dinged a second later.

Yummy! Enjoy!

A few minutes later, a big bull was led into the small pen and the gate clanged shut. Even over the noise of the crowd, she could hear the animal bellowing. His huge head snapped back and forth as if seeking a target.

Nash climbed up on the rail next to the bull and slapped its hindquarters. The bull bucked up, kicking the railing. Her heart raced. *He's not going to get on that bull, is he?* She clenched her hands together to keep from racing to the pen and yanking him down.

Another cowboy climbed up on the rail, and Nash was pointing at something on the bull. He clapped the other man on the back, then climbed down, stepped back as other hands stepped forward. He nodded at something, and his Stetson bobbed up and down. She wished she could see his face.

A few seconds later, he joined the line of men at the fence, and they watched the door open, then started hollering. She tore her eyes from Nash to the action in the arena. Riveted, she watched as the cowboy bounced up and down on the bull's back as it tried to toss the rider off.

Suddenly, the bull seemed to jump in the air and whirl around at the same time, and the man was flung off. The bull kept stampeding, heading straight for the cowboy lying in the dust. A couple of clowns raced out and grabbed the cowboy, helped him hobble to the side to safety.

She wrenched her eyes from the scene back to Nash. He stood apart from the other cowboys now, staring at the arena. His shoulders slumped, and he jammed his hands in his pockets, then kicked at something on the ground. He turned around and headed back to the stands, but the excitement that had been in his steps before was gone.

Not wanting him to see her watching him, she opened the program they'd bought on the way in and pretended to be reading.

"You rode bulls?"

"How'd you know?"

"Well, Jimmy asked if you'd give the rider pointers."

He tugged on his hat so it sat even lower, shadowing his eyes. "Yeah. I did."

"Is that what those buckles on your bookcase are for?"

The announcer interrupted whatever Nash was going to say, and another bull and rider was let out with a clang. It was like a train wreck. She wanted to squeeze her eyes shut tight and not watch, but she couldn't tear her gaze away.

Next to her, Nash shifted, and his left hand clenched

on his thigh. Habit had her sliding her hand on his leg and massaging it. He grabbed her hand to still it.

"She leaned closer to him. "Are you in pain?"

"Little bit."

"Then let me do my thing."

"Not here," he said, his voice gritty.

"You'd rather sit there in pain?"

His jaw clenched. "I'm fine."

"Then put your arm around me like I really am your date. If anyone sees me rubbing your leg, they'll just think I can't keep my hands off you."

He hesitated, and she didn't think he'd do it, but he finally lifted his left arm and curled it around her shoulders, tucking her even closer to his warm body. Darts of pleasure pinged through her. Felt good to be held like that. But the pleasure was followed by a twinge of guilt. *Rob.* She slid her hand back on his thigh and massaged the tight muscles until they finally gave a little and relaxed.

His thumb drifted slowly back and forth on her upper arm, and she peeked up at him. But his eyes were trained on the action in the arena. At least the tight brackets of pain around his mouth had loosened.

As she swung her gaze back toward the center arena, she glimpsed several cowboys against the fence watching them, grinning. One of them detached from the line and climbed up the railing again, handed a piece of paper to Nash, then climbed back down.

Honestly, did no one use the stairs here?

Nash removed his arm from her, and she was surprised at the spurt of disappointment. He unfolded the piece of paper, and she saw it was a flyer for a barbecue and dance following the rodeo. Crumpling it up, he started to toss it to the floor, but she stopped him.

"Let's go for a little while, okay?" she said to him.

"You don't really want to, do you?"

"Sure, might be fun."

"Why?"

"These are your friends, aren't they?"

"Yeah, some."

She nudged his shoulder. "It'll do you good to get your mind off things, talk rodeo with friends. Besides, I haven't had barbecue in a while."

He glanced at her. "If you're sure."

She nodded.

They watched the rest of the events, then left the building. Heavy falling rain made them hurry, following the crowd to the next building for the barbecue. Getting in line for the food, several people stopped to talk to Nash, welcome him back from the Army. He seemed to relax and actually smiled several times. She was glad she'd suggested they come. They filled up their plates and found a couple of spots at a partially filled table.

A band started playing a short time later, and people got up to dance. The cowboy who'd been thrown from the first bull—Rodney, she remembered—stopped at their table.

"Thanks for the pointers, Nash. I almost had him."

Nash set his bottle of beer down. "Sure thing. You'll get him next time."

Rodney glanced at her. "Aren't you and your girl gonna dance?"

Nash's mouth tightened, and he shook his head.

"Then do you mind if I ask her to dance?"

"She can do whatever she wants," he said.

Damn Rodney. If he hadn't come over, they could have gotten away. He'd thought he could handle coming to the dinner, but had forgotten about the unattached cowboys scooping up every available female.

Kelsey looked at him, hurt and confusion on her face. *Dammit.*

Then she smiled up at Rodney. "I'd love to dance. But it's been a while, so I'll apologize now for stepping on your toes." She took Rodney's hand and stood up, and they walked out on the dance floor.

Kelsey laughed as Rodney whirled her into a two-step, even as she stumbled over the steps. Rodney pulled her closer and whispered to her, and she nodded.

Fact was, he did like to dance, but with his damn leg blown off, he didn't dare try anything or he'd make a fool of himself.

The song blended into a different one, and another cowboy cut in, asked Kelsey to dance. Nash flagged down a passing waiter and got another beer.

The band kept playing and men kept cutting in to dance with Kelsey. His eyes followed her, and every time she laughed up at a man, he wanted to pound them into the ground. What was she thinking? She had a little girl at home, and a job to do.

She should be paying attention to me!

He slammed the bottle down and got up, wincing at the stiffness in his thigh, and he had to stop and balance himself. Which only made him madder.

He walked to the edge of the dance floor and waited until Kelsey and the current cowboy were close to him, and he tapped her on the shoulder. "We need to get you home, babe." And he grabbed her hand, pulling her from the dance floor. He stopped long enough for her to get her handbag, and they left the building.

It was still raining, even harder now, so he led her to

the covered walkway that would take them to the parking lot.

She yanked her hand away. "Would you tell me what's crawled up your butt and died?"

"You're not here to have fun and whoop it up with every cowboy you meet. You should be a little choosier with the men you flirt with. Or were you just trying to decide which one would take you home?"

"How dare you! I wasn't flirting, and I don't want any of those men. You practically threw me at them, you... you...*varmint*!"

It felt like a bucket of cold water had been thrown on his head, and he cracked a grin. "Varmint?"

She stared at him, arms crossed, tapping her toe on the ground. "It was the only thing I could come up with. I try not to cuss. But you make me so doggone mad."

"Yeah, but varmint?"

She stomped around him and headed toward the truck. He caught up to her and took her hand, but she yanked it away again. He had to impress on her how bad he'd messed up and knew it. Getting in front of her, he lightly grasped her upper arms and held her still. "I'm really sorry. Truly. I just got—"

"Got what?"

He shook his head, embarrassed to put it into words.

"Nash, tell me, please," she said, her voice low and husky.

"It just looked like you were having a lot of fun, and I wished it had been with me." He continued on, heading to end of the walkway. They'd get wet, but at this point he just wanted to get out of there.

But she tugged on his back pocket, making him stop. He couldn't face her, not now.

"In all honesty, I wish it had been you out there, too."

Had she really just said that?

"You do?" He turned around.

Her cheeks were pink in the glow from the lights. She nodded. "I thought it would be a fun evening for you to be with your friends. Instead you sat by yourself and everyone was afraid to talk to you. Why?"

"It's one thing to be around my family, who knew I'd been injured. But another to be back around these people I used to compete with. And now I can't—" He rubbed his jaw. "I realized tonight I won't ever be able to do normal things."

"Yes you will. Just might have to make adjustments."

"Like ride a bull?"

"Probably not… But do you want to?"

"Naw, I'm too old. Besides…" He shrugged. "It doesn't matter now. I'll never be the man I used to be."

Her mouth opened, but a door banged and a flood of people poured out of the building.

He grabbed her hand. "Come on. We'll have to make a run for it in this rain."

"Okay, but I'm driving."

"Why?"

"You may think I was out on the floor whooping it up, but I saw how much you had to drink. I'm driving."

Anger bubbled up and spewed forth. "I can drive."

"Maybe you can hold your alcohol, but it's storming, and your reaction time is slowed."

"No it's—"

She grabbed his arm. "Do you really want to be the one responsible for not getting me home to my daughter?"

Shit. Direct hit to his heart.

Men—good men—had died on his watch. He'd never let anything happen to her.

Reaching into his pocket, he wrenched the keys out and slapped them into her hand.

They hurried as fast as they could, given his leg, but still got drenched by the time they reached his truck. He opened the driver door and helped her in, then got to his door and climbed in. He reached behind the seat and pulled out a towel and blanket. "Might be kinda musty, but it's better than nothing."

He dried his face off, then pulled the blanket more tightly around Kelsey. She looked up at him, and his throat clogged.

He had to kiss her.

Now.

He leaned forward, kissed the corner of her mouth where her freckle sat. "I'm sorry."

Her breath hitched, and he was so damn happy when she turned her head just enough to meet his mouth. He pulled her closer, but a bright flash of lightning lit the sky, followed immediately by a loud crack of thunder.

Reluctantly he let her go, knew they needed to get on the road back to the ranch. It'd be a long ride in this weather, but he wanted to get her home.

To his cabin, if she'd go with him.

Another bright flash of lightning close by lit the sky, followed by an even louder crack of thunder. She flinched and pulled the blanket tighter around her. He glanced at her, concerned at her pale face. He reached for her hand. "You okay?"

She shook her head. "I hate thunderstorms."

"We'll be fine. Just take your time."

"My husband died in a storm like this." Her voice quavered.

"I'm sorry. We can just wait out the storm right here." He kept hold of her hand.

She shook her head and sat up straighter. "I want to get home." Pulling her hand free, she stuck the key in the ignition and started the engine. The parking lot was mostly empty now, and she maneuvered slowly across the bumpy gravel.

The wipers were going ninety miles a minute, but were still no match for the rain. Lightning arced through the sky to the ground, and it was so close it looked as if they would catch on fire if it struck them.

Kelsey screamed, and the truck fishtailed across the road, heading straight for a huge tree at the side of the road.

She got control and was able to stop the truck just before they hit the tree. His heart hammered against his chest, and he turned to see her slumped over, her head on the steering wheel.

Unbuckling his seat belt, he scooted as close as he could to her, pulling her into his arms. "Are you hurt? Did you hit your head?"

She shook her head and looked up at him. "Just scared. I thought I wouldn't stop in time." She pulled away to look out the front window. "That's a big tree."

It was safe to grin since she wasn't looking at him. "Yup."

Looking down at her watch, then back at him, she scrubbed her hands over her face. "Think we can get home?"

"No. I know you want to, but I don't think we should risk it." He rubbed his chin on her wet hair. "You won't let me drive, and you're exhausted. I wouldn't want to take a chance with this weather even if I hadn't had a few beers. Lots worse than I expected."

"So we're stuck here in the storm?"

"Not necessarily. I say we go back into town and see if we can find a motel and spend the night."

"Separate rooms?"

"Up to you."

She nodded and pulled her phone out of her handbag, tilted it to the light. "No service."

"We can call your mom when we get to town, okay?"

Starting the ignition again, she reversed and got them turned around, then slowly drove back into Billings. No Vacancy signs were posted all up and down the main road. Then he spied a B and B on a side street and she pulled into their lot. He climbed out and limped inside, where an older woman greeted him at the counter.

"Looks like you got caught in the rain. Do you need a room?"

It was tempting, but for Kelsey's sake, he reluctantly shook his head. "Two, just overnight."

The woman shook her head. "Sorry, hon, I only have one room left, and it's the honeymoon suite."

He winced and glanced outside the window and could barely make out Kelsey huddled against the driver-side door. "I'll take it. Be right back." How would she react?

Hurrying back through the rain, he opened her door and gently helped her out, then hustled her inside. She shivered in his arms, and his concern ratcheted up.

The older woman took one look at Kelsey and tsked. "You poor thing. Here's the key, and I'll bring up some extra towels and blankets. You go on up and get her out of those wet clothes. There's a bathrobe for each of you on the back of the bathroom door. Now go on."

"Thank you, ma'am. Do you mind bringing some hot tea or coffee?"

"I'll be right up."

He took the key and half carried Kelsey up the two

flights of steps. His thigh burned, but he couldn't think about that now. He had to get her warm. Unlocking the door, he walked them into a big bedroom. "Sorry. This is the only room they have available."

"O-o-k-kay," she said, her teeth chattering.

He led her to the chair by the fireplace and turned to make a fire. Luckily it was a gas fireplace. While he preferred the old-fashioned way of building a fire, for once he was grateful for modernization. He turned the key and got the fire going.

"Kelsey, honey, you need to get out of those wet clothes, okay? Come on, there's a robe for you in the bathroom."

She nodded and went into the bathroom and shut the door.

A knock sounded at the door, and he opened it to the proprietor, standing there with a tray. "I brought hot tea and cookies. And some brandy. You looked like you could use it. If there's anything you need, just ring down to the desk."

"Thank you, ma'am. I appreciate it."

He closed the door and put the tray on the table, then poured a shot of brandy and slugged it down. Fire burned all the way to his gut, but he was grateful for it.

A few minutes later, the bathroom door opened and she walked out, shrouded head to toe in a fluffy white bathrobe.

"Feel better?" He gulped, quickly looking everywhere but at her.

"Yes, a lot better. You get in there now."

He saluted her and hustled around her, closed the door behind him. Shucking his wet clothes, he pulled on the thick robe, dismayed to see how small it was on him. He'd just have to make sure he held it closed. Opening the door, he almost slammed it shut again. Kelsey sat by the fire, running a comb through her long dark hair.

She turned her head around to glance at him, the comb stilling in her hair. She suddenly faced the fire again, but her shoulders shook.

"What's wrong?" He hurried over to her, worried something had made her cry.

A laugh burst out of her, and she pointed to him.

He looked down and saw one good leg, and the prosthetic metal leg, still sporting one of Maddy's bandages. Heat bloomed in his chest and he bared his teeth. Arrows pinged at his heart. The one person who he thought would never laugh at him...at his leg—

She stood up and held her arms wide, then flapped her hands so the bathrobe sleeves drooped down over her wrists. "I must have gotten the wrong robe. Yours is too small, and mine's way too big!"

Her laughter shut down his hurt and anger. She was laughing over the robes?

He looked at himself in the mirror, then at her, and grinned. "Yeah, I think you did get mine."

"Like the three bears story."

Stepping closer, he picked up a lock of her dark hair and curled it around his finger. "I'd call you Goldilocks, but your hair's much prettier than hers." Damn, he hadn't meant to sound like that.

Her laughter stopped abruptly, and she stared at his chest. "I'll just go in the bathroom and hand it out to you. You can give me that one."

And she fled to the bathroom, closing the door behind her. Then it opened again, and her hand emerged, holding the robe. He slid his off and handed it to her, then pulled on the bigger one.

A few minutes later she came out, clutching the neck of the robe closed.

"Do you need to call your mom?"

"I used the landline while you were changing. Hope that's okay. I couldn't get through on my cell."

"Sure."

The stilted silence bothered him. "Do you want some tea?"

"I have some. Thanks."

He looked at the queen-size bed, then at the sofa against the window. "We should probably get some sleep." He headed toward the sofa.

"No, you take the bed," she said. "I fit better on the couch."

"I wouldn't be much of a gentleman if I let you do that." Suddenly, her words to Mindy echoed back at him. *Some women don't always want a gentleman.* He remembered what they'd been doing when she said it.

"I insist. You need to rest, and rest your leg. It'll be easier on the bed, won't it?"

She had a point, but he wasn't going to change his mind.

"Look, this is ridiculous. We can share the bed."

Her head shot up, and she froze.

"I promise I won't try anything." He held up two fingers. "Scout's honor."

She frowned. "Were you really a Scout?"

He grinned. "Nope. But we can pretend I was."

Laughing, she rolled her eyes. "Okay, but you promised, remember?"

Pulling the covers back, he sat on the left side of the bed and started to lie down.

"You need to take it off."

He stilled, ready to disagree.

"Don't argue, please. You've had a busy day, and I know your leg has to be hurting."

Gritting his teeth, he removed it. The pressure eased, and his leg did feel better, but it was still a disturbing shade of red.

She walked in front of him, holding a tube. "Can I take a look? I have some lotion so I can give you a massage."

His body tightened. He really wanted her hands on him, but didn't know if he could actually be that Boy Scout if she touched him. "You're tired, too. You need sleep."

"I wouldn't be a very good therapist if I let you be in pain, would I?" She opened the top and squirted lotion into her palm, then rubbed her hands together. "Come on, lie down."

He slid in and held the robe down as much as he could. She sat next to him on the bed and smoothed her hands over his thigh, moving higher, then lower.

It had gotten to be torture every time she massaged his leg. It was even worse now knowing they were both naked under the robes. He grew even harder and finally had to sit up and grab her hand, pry it off him. "It's good now. Thanks."

"Are you sure?"

He nodded, then yanked the covers up and flung an arm over his eyes.

"Did I hurt you?"

"No," he said, the word almost strangling in his throat.

The bed dipped as she climbed in and lay down.

Oh geez.

He forced himself to relax, just like he used to when in the Army. He'd never had to concentrate so hard. *Dammit, don't think about being hard.*

The sheets from her side of the bed rustled. "I'm sorry for whatever I did to hurt you."

"You didn't do anything."

"Then why are you mad?"

He rolled toward her, the ache in his damn thigh intensifying. "Because this." He cupped her cheeks and kissed her, devouring her mouth, drowning in the taste of her.

He kissed her until he couldn't take the pain any longer and had to force himself back, ripping his mouth from hers. "That's why. I want you so bad and I can't have you."

"Why can't you have me?" she whispered.

He slapped his thigh. "How can I make love to you when I'm half a man?"

Chapter Eleven

She shot up in bed and grabbed his hand, holding it to her chest. "Is that really what you think?"

His mouth opened, but no words came out.

"You're not half a man, but you are an idiot. You were injured, severely, which is why I'm here. To help you adapt to a new way of life, to compensate in other ways for what you used to do."

"Even sex?" he asked, trying to be flippant.

She rolled over and snapped the light off, drew the covers up and left him floundering for a way to apologize to her.

"I'm sorry. I never meant to imply anything untoward. I haven't been with anyone for a long time. A very long time. For obvious reasons. No woman would want me this way."

"Then the women you've met are very shallow. And idiots."

He grinned. She didn't hold back what she thought, did she?

She rolled back over and sat up. "And for the record..." She kissed him, shocking him as her lips did crazy things to his libido. "I want you too, and it frustrates me to no end."

She wanted him?

He reached over to the lamp and snapped it on, turned back to face her. Her dark hair spread across her shoulders, and the robe gaped open enough to show her very sexy collarbone.

Her breath hitched, and he wondered if she was afraid.

But she didn't know that's exactly how he felt right now.

He cupped her cheek, using his thumb to caress the delicate skin. Easing forward, he kissed her, taking his time, learning the contour of her lips again. She sighed, and he took it deeper, lightly touching her tongue with his.

She arched closer to him, and he felt her hand slip inside the robe to caress his chest.

He froze, the image of his scars screaming a reminder that his body was marred. Moving back, he grabbed her hand and pulled it away. "We shouldn't do this."

"Why?"

"Because…" He racked his brain for an excuse that wouldn't sound vulnerable, but that's just how he felt right now. He couldn't stand rejection.

Shoving back the covers, Kelsey scooted around to sit on her knees, facing him. "You're not going to stop now. Not when you've had me on the edge for days with your kisses, the way you've touched my body."

"But *your* body is perfect," he snapped.

"Nash," she murmured, cupping his cheeks and kissing him. "You forget I've already seen your body, or most of it. I've got my own scars—they're just on the inside." She untied the belt on his robe, and he fought to hold the edges together.

But she kept going, opening the robe, sliding down the bed to lie next to him. He squeezed his eyes shut, dreading seeing her face when she saw him up close. The touch of her lips on his chest almost made him jackknife up. Every drop of blood in his head raced south as she continued touching him.

The robe gaped wide-open now, and he didn't even have the sheet to shield his missing leg from her.

Why were they doing this? It couldn't end well, for either of them. She had a child to consi—

Crap. Baby.

"Stop. Kelsey, you have to stop." He grabbed her hands before they wandered much lower. He wanted her. Wanted her touch, wanted her heart, wanted all of her.

"Why?"

"I don't have any protection."

She smiled, her eyes looking all sultry and seductive. "You forget. This is the honeymoon suite."

"So?"

She reached in the pocket of her bathrobe and pulled out a handful of foil-wrapped packages. "Full service B and B. Gotta love 'em." She tossed the condom packets onto his chest and stared down at him, his erection aching for her attention.

And when her fingers wrapped around him, silky and smooth, he worried he wouldn't last long enough to use a condom.

She kept surprising him, and he wanted her so bad. The logistics of his situation was like a bucket of cold water thrown over him. He couldn't make love to her the way he wanted to.

"Stop thinking," she said, kneeling on the bed next to him.

"Huh?"

"You're suddenly miles away from this room. What's going on?"

Heat crawled up his chest, suffusing his face. How

could he explain to this beautiful, vibrant woman what he was going through?

"Talk to me."

He shook his head.

"Then touch me." She untied the belt of her robe and shrugged it off.

The breath backed up in his lungs.

"Touch me," she whispered, and damned if she didn't look vulnerable, as well.

SHE'D BARED HERSELF to him.

What if he rejected her?

She'd had a child, wasn't all that young anymore. Rob had liked her curves, but she had a weakness for Rocky Road ice cream. And it showed. She wanted Nash, and it was such a shock that she was going after him. But he was like chocolate cake, ice cream and the best champagne, and she craved him.

He sat up and pulled off his robe, tossed it to the floor. Scars be damned, he still had a gorgeous body, and she wanted him with an acute ache.

She hesitated a second, then put her hands on his broad shoulders, put her leg on his other side so she faced him.

They stared at each other, then he pulled her close, kissed her neck. Sharp arrows of desire twanged through her, and she held his head in place. Sensations flooded her, and she wanted him—all of him—now. But didn't want it to end too soon.

He slid a finger down her stomach, and she caught her breath, trying not to scream.

She leaned sideways and picked up a foil packet, tore it open and handed it to him. "Now. Please, now."

He sheathed himself, and she sank down, only to have

him fill her up. Her eyes closed, and she lost herself in the feel of him.

"You okay, babe?"

She opened her eyes. "Yes," she breathed.

Rain still pelted the windows, and thunder rumbled. But inside their cozy cocoon, she let herself go and drowned in him.

SOMETHING NUDGED KELSEY and she woke up, disoriented. The normal night-light in her bathroom wasn't on. She turned over and her muscles screamed in protest. It all came flooding back—she'd slept with Nash. Squinching her eyes closed, the recriminations assailed her.

Moaning interrupted her thoughts, however, and she looked at the other side of the bed. Nash sat up on the side of the bed, his back hunched over.

"What's wrong?" she asked, turning on the lamp.

"Damn. I didn't mean to wake you."

"Are you in pain?"

"Cramp in my thigh. Bad one."

She scrambled out of bed and searched for her robe in the shadows. Finally finding it, she hurried to his side of the bed and pulled a chair in front of him.

"Okay, try to slow your breathing."

His fingers dug into his quads, and sweat beaded on his forehead. She rubbed her hands together to warm them, then laid them on his upper leg. Massaging deep, she kept doing it until the muscles relaxed, and his hands unclenched.

"Thanks. Feels better now."

"Good. Now lie facedown."

"Why?"

"You need to relax. I want to give you a rubdown."

"You don't need to do that. You've had a long day."

"Just do it, please." She grabbed the lotion from the table while he complied and lay facedown, the sheet pulled up to his waist.

She squeezed lotion into her hands and rubbed them together, then started massaging his shoulders. The knots were hard as rocks, and she couldn't help but worry about him. "Do you get cramps very often?"

He shrugged under her hands. "Most nights."

"You should have told the doctor. Call him when we get back, okay?"

"Yeah."

His muscles finally loosened up, and she soothed her hands over his back, not as a therapist now, but as a woman appreciating a man's body. His breathing deepened. *Must have fallen back asleep, thank goodness.*

She'd been wrong to sleep with him, but she already craved him again. Forcing herself to stand up, she moved the chair back into place and looked out the window. The rain had stopped, and she hoped they'd be able to get out of town before too long.

She debated spending the rest of the night on the sofa, but was too tired. Leaving her robe on, she got back into bed as quietly as she could and turned the light off. It had been a lot of years since she'd shared her bed with anyone. Nash had taken up part of her side, and she scrunched over as much as possible.

Finally relaxing, she'd just closed her eyes when he groaned. "No," he said, his voice harsh.

"Nash," she whispered, touching his shoulder.

He yanked away from her, seemed to be moving the covers around.

"Wake up," she said. "Nash, wake up. Come on, honey." She stroked a hand over his chest, hoping to soothe him.

His eyes fluttered open, then focused on her. "What happened?"

"You were having a nightmare." She smoothed a damp lock of hair away from his forehead, felt the heat radiating from him. Clutching the robe tight, she hurried into the bathroom and ran a washcloth under cold water, then brought it back to him. He'd leaned forward, his breath heaving, hands covering his face.

Sitting next to him on the bed, she tried to pull his hands away.

"Leave me alone."

She set the cool washcloth on the back of his neck and went to the tray the B and B owner had brought them the night before. The tea was cold, but the brandy would work. She poured him a shot and brought it back to him, nudged his hand with the tumbler.

He spared a glance at her, but took the glass and downed it in one gulp. "More." He shoved the glass at her, but she hesitated. "Please," he said, voice still hoarse.

"What were you dreaming?"

"Not telling you."

"It might help if you get it out of your head."

"No."

"Why?" she persisted, hoping he'd tell her.

"If I tell you, will you give me another drink?"

She hesitated, but it might be the only way to get him talking. "Tell me."

"Recurring nightmare. The night my unit was attacked, and the bomb blew my leg off. And my men died. Satisfied?" He shoved the glass at her.

This time she took it and poured another one, handed it to him, which he downed faster than the first.

"I'm sorry. I know that doesn't help. It was a war," she said quietly, her heart aching for him. No wonder he was so angry and bitter. She hadn't realized how much guilt he felt at being the only survivor.

"You weren't there."

"Nash, you can't keep going on like—"

"Bring me the bottle."

"Talk to me. Please."

"No."

"Will you think about talking to someone?"

"Give me the damn bottle."

"You need to get some sleep."

"It'll help me sleep."

"Is this how you get to sleep every night?"

"None of your business."

"The hell it's not!"

He stared up at her, his eyes narrowed. "Give me the bottle."

"Get it yourself."

"I'd have to put the blasted leg on, then take it back off."

"Don't care. I'm not going to enable your drinking." She stalked away and grabbed her pillow and a blanket, then plunked on the sofa and closed her eyes.

A minute later she heard a grunt and cracked her eyelids open. Nash had picked up his prosthesis and had hooked it around the leg of the coffee table the tray was sitting on and pulled it toward him. She stuffed her face into the pillow so she wouldn't laugh at his ingenuity.

But her humor didn't last long. He was using alcohol as a crutch. That would have to stop. She just had to find a way to make it happen.

Chapter Twelve

The ride back to the ranch was long, and not just because of the debris and ruts caused by the storm. The silence pressed on Nash, and he was ready to explode by the time they drove beneath the sign leading to the ranch.

Doubts and self-recriminations had assailed him the whole way home. Words tumbled through his head, but he'd never been one for giving speeches of any kind.

The main house loomed in front of them, and the front door opened. Bunny walked out onto the porch and waved at them with her good arm. He stopped the truck and Kelsey opened her window.

"You're home safe! Everything okay?"

No, ma'am, it isn't. I slept with your daughter last night. He just nodded.

"Good. You're just in time for breakfast."

"I'm not really hungry, Mom. I just want to get home and change clothes. Is Maddy with you or at day care?"

"She's here with us. Please come inside, both of you."

Angus walked up behind Bunny and put his arm around her shoulder. "Nash, y'all come in. Breakfast is ready, and your brothers are here."

"Dad—"

"Come in. Now," Angus ordered, and led Bunny back into the house, leaving the door open.

"Well, I guess we better go in," Nash said, shutting off the engine.

They got out of the truck and went inside, the noise of the whole family together hitting him like a wall. Maddy sat on Hunter's lap, giggling as he played patty-cake with her. But as soon as she saw Kelsey and Nash, she scooted down and ran, throwing her chubby little arms around her mother's legs.

"How's my baby girl? I missed you last night!" She picked Maddy up and they sat at the dining table.

"I missed you, Mommy! But I had fun, too."

"You did? What'd you do?"

"Uncle Kade and Toby played games with me, then we ate popcorn and watched movies!"

"*Uncle* Kade?" Nash asked, looking at Kelsey as he sat across from her.

She shrugged, then passed the platter of bacon to him.

Angus stood up and cleared his throat, then walked around the table to Bunny's chair. He put a hand on her shoulder. "Bunny and I wanted you all here today to give you some good news."

Bunny beamed up at him, then laid her hand on Kelsey's arm. "Angus and I are engaged!"

In an instant, the room went silent.

"You're what?" Kelsey croaked. Her eyebrows had climbed up her forehead, and he knew his had to match.

Maybe he hadn't heard right.

"We're getting married!" Bunny exclaimed.

Okay, heard it right the first time.

"But…but…you barely know each other," Kelsey sputtered, her face pale.

"What the he—" He glanced at Maddy, then cleared his throat. "What the heck are you two thinking? Kelsey and her family will be moving on before too long."

Out of the corner of his eye, he saw Kelsey's head whip around. He felt like her eyes were drilling into him. What? Did she think he'd propose with hearts and flowers just because they slept together?

"Oh, Nash. Now I know Kelsey has been working you hard in therapy, but you're not ready to run us off just yet, are you?" Bunny asked. "Besides, your father and I are in love."

He glanced at his dad, and dang if he didn't have a look of tenderness on his face.

"I can't believe—" An elbow jabbed into his side and he glared at Kade.

"Hey, Toby. Why don't you take Maddy out back and show her the new kittens?"

Maddy squealed.

Toby popped up out of his chair. "Come on! I'll race ya!"

Their feet thudded across the wood floor and through the doorway, then the door slammed behind them.

His brothers all spoke at once.

"Enough!" his dad roared. The old man might be well into his sixties, but he was still vital and still head of the family.

Silence settled over the room, and his dad spread his feet, fisted his hands on his hips. "You boys—"

Bunny slipped her hand through his dad's arm and pulled him down beside her. "I know you all have some concerns," she said, her voice quiet and gentle. "But you should understand. Your father and I have been alone for a long time. We've fallen in love and want to spend the rest of our lives together. Haven't you ever fallen for someone, then wanted more than anything to be with that person?" She glanced directly at him, then at her daughter.

Nash felt heat creeping up his chest. Did she know? Could she tell?

Hunter cleared his throat, a smile crossing his face. "Well, I guess congratulations are in order." He stood and kissed Bunny on the cheek. "Welcome to the family."

Each of his brothers followed after him. He glanced up to see his dad scowling at him, which guilted him into pushing his chair back. Just as he started to stand, a cramp in his thigh struck, and he grunted, falling back onto the chair. Waves of nausea rose from his stomach, and he was afraid he'd hurl in front of everyone.

A chair screeched across the floor, and he slitted his eyes open enough to see Kelsey hurrying around the table. She crouched next to him and started rubbing his thigh. Even though the pain was really intense this time, all he could think about was her tending to him the night before.

In her robe.

Naked under her robe.

He shoved her hand away and stood, grabbing the edge of the table for support. Bracing himself on the table, he hobbled around to Bunny and kissed her cheek. "Best wishes," he mumbled, then walked with measured steps to the door, ignoring the pain, and ignoring the hard truth that just walking across the floor was a struggle. He wished like hell he could ignore the self-loathing he felt for being only half a man.

Behind him, he heard Bunny ask, "What happened yesterday? Is Nash all right?"

He closed the door, cutting off Kelsey's reply. Another knife-sharp cramp struck him, and he nearly went down. Grabbing the railing, he punched his thigh, over and over. The pain ratcheted through him. *Will this ever end?*

"Want a lift home?" Wyatt asked.

Pride warred with the need to get to his own cabin and be alone. He nodded, and Wyatt lent a shoulder to help him down the steps, then opened the passenger door to Nash's truck.

He sank down onto the seat and slammed the door shut, handed the keys over and shut his eyes.

"Wanna talk?" Wyatt asked.

"Nope. Don't want to talk about her."

"Her? You mean Kelsey? I was talking about your injury."

Crap. He looked out the window and wished he hadn't opened his mouth.

"You never said what happened over there. All we know is your unit was ambushed, and you were injured trying to save your team."

They pulled up in front of his cabin, and he got out, bracing himself on the truck. Tried to put weight on his leg, only to have the pain again.

"Would you just wait a damn minute? I'll help you." Wyatt slammed his door and came around the side of the truck.

He let his brother take most of his weight as they walked inside and to the couch. "Thanks, bro." Waiting for Wyatt to leave, he instead heard glasses clinking.

Wyatt sat down in the chair next to the sofa, plunked a bottle of whiskey and two glasses down on the coffee table.

"Kinda early, isn't it?"

"You turning down a drink?" Wyatt unscrewed the top and poured them each a hefty glass.

"Hell no."

"We could use the excuse of toasting Dad and Bunny." Wyatt raised his glass in the air, and Nash leaned forward enough to clink his against it.

"So, you want to talk?"

What could he say?

It was his fault seven men had died?

He could still hear the bomb screaming overhead, taste the acrid mixture of gunpowder and blood.

Raising his glass, he swallowed the whiskey, relishing the few seconds it drowned out the noise and taste of death.

THE DAY HAD turned chilly, and Kelsey looked up at the heavy clouds gathering above. Back home in Florida, it was warm almost all the way through Thanksgiving, sometimes even Christmas. It couldn't snow in August, could it? She shivered, wishing she'd brought a jacket with her.

Pulling a box of food out of the passenger seat, she shut the door and mentally pulled up her big girl panties. Nash would most likely be in a nasty mood. Of course he was always in a bad mood, but pain and anger at his father would make him even testier than usual. But there had been a few times he'd been fun to be around.

Raising her fist, she knocked, then waited for him to answer. Nothing. She knocked again and glanced behind her to make sure she'd really seen his truck. Maybe he'd fallen asleep?

Giving it one more shot, she knocked again.

"Go away," he hollered from inside.

Okay, bad mood it was.

She tried the doorknob, but it was locked. Good thing Kade had given her a spare key when she said she wanted to check on Nash. Inserting the key into the door handle, she unlocked it and shoved the door open, then peered into the dim light of the main room.

"What do you want?"

Searching through the gloom, she saw him lying on the couch. "I thought you might be hungry." She bit her lip. "And I wanted to check on you."

"Well, ain't that neighborly of you."

She straightened her shoulders, refusing to let him get to her. "Mrs. Green made some of your favorite foods." Setting the box on the counter, she lifted a covered container out and set it on the counter. Searching through a couple of drawers, she found the silverware and napkins.

"Not hungry."

She didn't say anything, just took the cover off the plate and gathered things together, then walked to the couch. The amazing aroma of fried chicken blended with the gravy swamping the mashed potatoes, and her own mouth watered.

A half-empty bottle of whiskey sat on the coffee table, along with two glasses. She sat down in the chair next to the couch and balanced the plate on her knees.

"I said I'm not hungry."

"Good. Then I guess this plate is mine. I'm not going to let this food go to waste. Not when I've heard how good Mrs. Green's fried chicken is."

As she lifted a piece of golden-brown crispy chicken toward her mouth, she heard a low grumble. Then another long grumble. Finally realized it was coming from Nash's stomach.

He sat up. "Oh, all right. Give it to me."

She bit the inside of her cheek to keep from laughing and handed the plate and silverware over to him. Luckily Mrs. Green had packed two containers, so she hurried over to the box on the counter and grabbed the other one, along with another set of silverware. On her way back to the chair, she turned the end table lamp on, and a soft glow chased away some of the darkness.

Now that she could see him, she noticed dark smudges beneath his eyes and lines of pain bracketing his mouth. She wouldn't say anything now, wanted him to finish his meal first.

Again lifting a chicken breast, this time she took a bite, and nearly swooned as the flavors exploded on her tongue. She closed her eyes and savored another bite, then another. Opening her eyes again, she picked up her fork to scoop up mashed potatoes, but stopped when she saw him staring at her, his own fork hovering above his nearly empty plate.

"What? Do I have chicken grease on my face?"

"No, you were moaning."

"Oh. Sorry."

"You moaned like that last—" He stopped talking, then shoveled in the last bites of mashed potatoes.

Last... Embarrassment flooded her when she realized he'd been talking about last night.

Which brought back all the pleasure he'd given her. Just remembering the way he'd touched her had her skin burning. Maybe coming here now hadn't been such a good idea, but she'd been worried about him.

Finishing her food, she made sure to stifle her moans. She stood, took his plate, then walked into the kitchen. After rinsing the dishes in the sink, she took the pie out of the box.

"Mrs. Green sent a cherry pie for dessert."

"She's too good to me."

"She loves you, and all of your brothers," she said, walking back to the couch.

He looked up at her. "Don't I get some of that pie?"

"Not till I check your leg."

A scowl crossed his face. "You don't need to."

"Yes I do. You were in the most pain I've seen you in

up to now." She put her hands on her hips and glared at him. "So do you want to go change into shorts, or shall I take your jeans off here?"

As soon as she said the words, she wanted to yank them back.

Too late. A sly grin crossed his face, and he leaned back against the pillow and crossed his hands behind his head. "Go ahead, babe."

She slitted her eyes. So he was daring her now, was he? *Fine.*

Bending over, she reached for his pant leg, then realized she'd never get the denim pulled up far enough.

He moved his arm, pulling his T-shirt up enough to bare his belt buckle and a hint of steely abs.

Gritting her teeth, she reached for his buckle, but her hand trembled just a bit. She really hoped he hadn't seen it.

Pretend you're working on a cadaver back in med school. Ignore the heat of his body, the muscles, his skin...

The rasp of his zipper echoed loudly through the room as she lowered it. She couldn't help but be turned on. *Think cadaver!*

She reached for the waistband of his jeans, and he lifted up so she could pull them down.

His white briefs couldn't contain his arousal.

Oh, have mercy.

Jerking back, she bumped into the coffee table and lost her balance. He grabbed her arm and kept her from falling, then pulled her down on top of him.

"Kelsey..." he murmured, then leaned forward and kissed her.

He licked her lip until she opened to him. She tasted a

hint of whiskey on his tongue, and pushed away. "You've been drinking."

"Only enough to dull the pain."

"This isn't a good idea."

"It was last night."

"No, it wasn't."

"You don't mean that," he whispered, sliding his hand under her shirt to caress her stomach.

"Yes I do," she said, and shoved away.

"He's dead. You're alive," Nash snapped.

His words were a slap to her face.

"Have you ever been in love?" she asked, forcing the words out. "Love doesn't die when a loved one does."

He scrubbed a hand across his face. "Do you really think Rob would want you to be alone, and lonely, for the rest of your life?"

She crossed her arms across her middle, her shoulders hunching up. "You don't understand."

"Then help me understand. I…I care about you, Kelsey." He pulled her down to lie on top of him. It helped, not having to face him.

"It should have been me in that car." She forced the words out, reliving that horrible night when the police officer came to her door.

"Why?"

"I was supposed to go to the store for something, but I had a bad headache and asked Rob to go for me. He left, then never came home." She sniffled. "How can I move on and be happy when it's my fault?"

He didn't say anything, but his hand brushed through her hair, soothing her. "You know what I think?"

She shook her head, rubbing against him, listening to his heartbeat, sure and steady.

"I think we're two lonely people, still hurting from things that happened beyond our control."

Surprised, she sat up and stared at him. "Did you sneak off and see a counselor while I wasn't looking?"

He frowned. "Uh, no."

"It just sounds very counselorish."

"Is that bad?"

She gave a watery laugh. "No. Sounds like something I would have said."

He cupped her cheek and gazed into her eyes, as if he could see inside her soul.

She knew he wanted to kiss her, and she put her hand over his. "Oh, Nash. You make me feel things I haven't in a very long time. But you're my patient—"

His head dropped back and he huffed out a breath. "And what if I was your friend instead? Would you find some other excuse for us not to be together?"

She kept silent, battling her feelings on the inside.

Raising his head again, he caressed her cheek, then brushed a hand up and down her back. He nuzzled her neck, and she shivered.

"Nash…" she mumbled, reveling in his touch. Every slide of his hand made her tingle, and she wanted him with a ferocity that scared her. She knew he was right. Rob was gone, and she was still young. Her own mother had found someone to love even at her age.

His hand slid to her waistband and undid the buttons with ease. "You should wear skirts," he murmured in her ear, eliciting a shock wave through her body. "You've got killer legs."

She started to back away, but he grabbed her arm. "Don't." He tugged, and she moved closer, straddled his legs on the couch. Heat from his legs warmed her bottom, but it was uneven, his left leg feeling much warmer than the right.

"Nash, stop."

He kissed her, murmuring against her lips, "Don't you want me?"

"Your leg is too warm. We don't want infection to set in."

He sighed, then leaned back. "Go ahead. Have at it."

"Oh, I intend to, as soon as I get a look at your leg."

His mouth kicked up in a half grin, but he turned his head as she stretched the bandage away from his thigh. It didn't look red, just warm, the scars puckering his skin.

"Does it hurt right now?"

He shook his head. "The covering makes my leg hot and sweaty sometimes, but it's not hurting right now."

"Then let's take the prosthesis off for the night," she said, and reached for it.

He grabbed her hand. "Not yet. I want to feel whole again. At least while I make love to you."

Her heart beat faster at his words, and she moved her hands away, then slid them up to his T-shirt and pulled it off.

Pulling her close, he unbuttoned her blouse, and gazed at her chest as if she were a work of art. Licks of desire flamed from low in her belly outward, and it empowered her. That he would look at her—at *her*, the mother of a young child, a widow, in that way. Like a man looks at a woman he wants and thinks is sexy.

She slid her hands up his muscled arms, up his neck, finally to tangle her fingers in his short hair. Being outside so much had burnished the tips to golden brown, and the softness was a stark contrast to the hardness in him.

Since her husband had died, taking a part of her with him, she never thought she'd be with another man. And now here she was, again, about to be with this strong, vulnerable man.

She let her fingers drift down to his jawline, tipped his head up and kissed him, pouring all the things she wanted to say to him but was afraid to into the kiss. His fingers clenched on her hips, as if he was holding on for more than just sex.

A tremor ran through her body, shaking her to her core.

She held him close, her pounding heart echoing his own. He lay back, pulling her with him, and she nestled close to him, resting her cheek on his shoulder.

She loved the way he ran a hand down her spine, then cupped her butt.

She loved the way he turned his head just enough to kiss her forehead.

She loved...

Him.

Chapter Thirteen

Nash picked up the pillow and tossed it on the couch. He'd never look at that sofa the same way again. The things he and Kelsey had done on it, just an hour before...

His front door opened, and in walked Wyatt, followed by Kade, Hunter and Luke. He blew out a breath, grateful he'd refused to take his prosthesis off before Kelsey left, even if she had lectured him. And after great sex, too.

"What the hell do y'all want?"

Kade held up a round box. "Poker night."

Nash glared at his brothers as they made themselves at home. Wyatt set up the portable poker table that had been in the family for as long as he could remember. Luke rummaged through the bar cabinets, then brought glasses and whiskey to the table.

"What brought this on?" he asked, angry about his loss of privacy.

Kade shrugged. "Haven't done one since you've been home. Figured it was ten years past time for a boys' night, what with all these women invading the ranch."

Nash frowned. "You mean Kelsey and her family?"

"Yeah. Don't you feel it? Bunny's up at the lodge or Dad's house all the time now, making plans. Kelsey's here all the time, or with her daughter, cute as she is, roaming around."

"I don't see it that way. She's here to do a job—"

Kade plopped into a chair at the poker table. 'I don't believe it. You were pissed that Dad hired her to begin with. You crossing over to the dark side?"

"You sonuva—"

"We gonna play cards or yap all night?" Hunter asked, shuffling a deck of cards.

Nash gritted his teeth. "Just 'cause you hate women in general doesn't mean they're all like *her*."

Kade's eyes narrowed, and his face got stony.

Nash almost regretted bringing up Kade's ex-wife. They'd gotten married right before he shipped out, and he couldn't believe Kade had fallen for that calculating, cold woman. And from what Hunter had emailed him, she'd really done a number on Kade, and on Toby. Good thing she'd decided to leave when she did, although the divorce had been nasty, leaving Kade with a dim view of women in general.

"I'm not saying Kelsey, or Bunny, are like Sheila," Kade said, then slammed a shot of whiskey. "They just haven't been here very long, and already Dad's popped the question."

"Dad's been a widower a long time. Doesn't he deserve some happiness?" Hunter asked, and dealt the cards.

"Happiness? Sure. But what's Bunny in it for? And who's next?" Kade shrugged. "Better watch your back, Nash, or Kelsey might try the same thing with you."

"Geez, you really have gotten bitter, haven't you? Kelsey isn't like that."

"Just sayin'. She's a widow with a little girl to raise. And from that POS car she drives, she doesn't make a lot of money."

Heat flushed through Nash's body, and his fists clenched. But before he could say anything, Hunter flung his cards on the table, his face beet red. "Bull. She's one of the hardest-working women I know. Look who she has to work with!" He flung a thumb in Nash's direction, and it pissed him off even more. "No offense, bro." Hunter glanced at him, then turned his attention back to Kade.

"You sniffing around her, too?" Kade sneered.

Nash gripped the edge of the table, his fingers biting into the felt covering. He rose up from the chair, ready to fling the table out of the way and pummel first Hunter, then Kade.

She's mine, dammit. Had she really been flirting with Hunter right beneath his nose?

A hand came down on his arm, and he glanced at Wyatt, then flung it off. "Calm down and listen," his brother said so quietly Nash had to strain to hear it.

Sitting back down, he tuned in again to what Hunter was saying. "Anyone with a lick of sense can see she's focused on getting Nash healthy."

"Sure, so she can clear the field, get the job done, get her hooks into one of you."

Spots flashed across his vision, and Nash blinked hard, his stomach tightening. He shot up out of the chair, catching himself as a cramp burned through his thigh and the chair crashed behind him. He lunged around the table, determined not to show any weakness in front of his brothers, and grabbed Kade by the front of his shirt, yanking him up. "You don't talk about her that way," he growled.

He shoved his younger brother so hard he fell over the coffee table.

Kade started to get up, then looked down again. A bitter I-told-you-so smile crossed his face. "You still saying she's not trying to get something out of you?" he asked, then held up a pair of women's lacy blue underwear. "Unless you changed in the Army and these are yours, I think we know what she's been up to."

He grabbed them from Kade's hand and shoved them in his pocket. Almost blind with rage, he drew back, ready to punch Kade's lights out, teach him a lesson long past due.

"What in tarnation is goin' on here?" Angus thundered from the front door.

Everyone turned to look at their dad, freezing in place like wild bucks sensing danger. For several seconds, the room was as quiet as a Montana meadow after a heavy snowfall.

"Just a little misunderstanding, right guys?" Hunter said, always the peacemaker.

Nash dropped his arm. He'd have to kill Kade later. When there weren't so many damn witnesses.

Hunter reached a hand out to Kade and pulled him up.

Kade blew out a breath and rubbed the back of his neck. "I'm sorry, bro. I didn't mean any of it."

"Does this have something to do with that email from your ex?" Angus asked, looking at Kade.

Kade closed his eyes and his head dropped back. "Yeah."

Nash frowned. "What's she want? I didn't think you ever heard from her."

"I usually don't. But she crawled out of her snake pit, wanting her alimony increased."

"You're still paying her alimony? She left you, pal. You shouldn't be paying her a dime."

"Hey, it's worth it to keep her out of our lives."

No wonder Kade had walked into the cabin tonight with all that bitter venom bubbling under the surface. Nash felt for him, he really did, but the divorce had soured Kade's view of women for too many years.

Wyatt yanked a chair out and sat. "We playing cards or not?"

"Hey, Dad, were you looking for one of us?"

Angus hefted a box. "Bunny asked me to bring y'all some snacks." He set it on the kitchen island and unpacked bowls of chips and snacks, then turned around. 'Well, I'll let you boys get back to it."

Crap. Nash looked up at him, and dang if he didn't look like he felt left out. "You want in?" The words seemed to tumble from his mouth faster than a weed blowing across the desert.

Angus grinned, and hung his hat on the rack by the door. "What's the buy-in?"

Nash caught Wyatt's grimace before he turned his head. He'd bet anything Bunny had done this on purpose. "Fifty."

They sorted out bills and chips, then Wyatt shuffled the deck and dealt the cards.

"Shorty turned in his notice this morning," Angus said, tossing a chip on the table.

"First Curly, now Shorty?" Hunter asked.

"Guess they are both at retirement age," Kade said. "At least Curly's easy to replace now that Nash is home."

"We need to start looking for a new foreman. He and Helen will be leaving in two months, before their next grandchild is born," Angus said. "We can run an ad, but I'd rather see if there's someone we can promote who already knows the setup here. Any ideas?"

A few names were thrown around the table, most were vetoed. It'd be hard to replace Shorty, even if he was getting up in years.

"Whoever we hire needs to be willing to use the computer. Too much has been slipping through the cracks since Shorty refuses to use it. I'm always finding slips of paper with the chore list floating around," Kade said.

"Speaking of chores, I was out on a call at the Henderson ranch yesterday, saw a northeast section of fence was down," Luke said, then anted up. "Need to add it to the foreman's list."

"It's fixed," Wyatt said, then flipped in his own chips.

"Need to have Shorty start winterizing the chicken coops."

"Did it," Wyatt said.

"Tractor broke down in the southwest field, still needs to be towed in."

"Hauled it in before I came here." Watt reached behind him for the bowl of chips and grabbed a handful.

Nash looked up from his cards and studied Wyatt. He'd left home about the same time Nash had enlisted—hadn't finished high school, just up and left one night. Wyatt had finally come home recently, refused to talk about his time away from the ranch. Now that he was home, he'd pitched right in without being asked. He'd been picking up the slack for Shorty lately—maybe he'd be the right choice for foreman.

His younger brother had gotten in trouble a few times in school, had a rebellious streak a mile wide. Long dark hair, with a big chip on his shoulder—the girls had gone mad for him, and he'd had to beat them off with a stick. Although he hadn't tried too hard, if memory served correctly.

Looking down again at his cards, he folded his lousy hand and wondered what Kelsey was doing, then caught himself.

No use mooning about like a lovesick calf. He needed to keep his head in the game, not on how her dark-as-night hair gleamed in the sunlight, or how she felt moving against his body.

Damn. He had no business thinking about her this way—as if he wanted her to stay. *She's a widow with a little girl—last thing she needs is someone like me in her life.*

Chapter Fourteen

"But I wanna see the kitties!" Maddy wailed.

So not what Kelsey needed today. She was still reeling from her time with Nash the week before. A headache bloomed behind her eyes, and it was all she could do to hold on to her temper.

"Sweetie, I have to go to work for a few hours. We can't go up to see them right now, okay?"

Storm clouds passed over Maddy's face, and her normally sweet-tempered daughter pouted and crossed her chubby arms over her chest. "I don't care. I want to see them. Toby said I could help name them." She stomped her foot. "And I want to go. NOW."

Praying for patience, Kelsey wondered where this attitude was coming from all of a sudden. "It's so cold and rainy outside that I'll bet the kitties are snuggled up with their mommy, keeping warm." At least she hoped they were as she looked out the drizzle-covered window at the rain coming down fast and furious.

"I think it's nap time, but I promise we'll go later to see the kittens, okay? Come on, let's go." She picked her daughter up, which was getting harder every day, and took her to her bedroom. Setting Maddy on the floor, she pulled the covers back and waited for her to climb in to bed.

"Now you take a good nap, okay?" She kissed her plump little cheek, currently red and tearstained. "I love you."

"Love you, Mommy," Maddy said, still pouting, and pulled her favorite bear closer, clamped her eyes shut.

Hopefully the nap would restore her good nature.

Kelsey glanced at her watch, then hurried into the living room just as her mother walked in. "Mom, I have to run—I'm late for Nash's therapy. Maddy's taking a nap, and will hopefully be in a better mood later."

"She'll be fine. Just growing up. I seem to remember someone else who threw a tantrum about wanting to see the newborn foals when she was about Maddy's age."

Kelsey grinned. "I have no idea what you're talking about." She kissed her mother's cheek. "I'll be home as soon as I can."

She gathered up her bag, raincoat and umbrella, and headed out to her car. Getting in, she tried to start it, but it groaned and clunked. Closing her eyes, she prayed it would last just a little bit longer. A new car was not in her budget for a long time.

The engine finally caught, and she drove slowly through the storm to Nash's cabin. Pulling her resolve around her like a cloak, she swore to herself no more sex with him, as wonderful as it was. He was becoming too important to her, but with no future in sight, she couldn't just sleep with him.

He opened the door as she walked up to it. "We could have canceled the session. You shouldn't have driven over here in weather like this."

"We need to continue your sessions so you keep progressing. Just think of me as a mailman—neither rain, nor sleet, nor snow will keep me from my job."

"In that case, want to play post office?"

Laughter bubbled out of her. "You're incorrigible, aren't you?"

A COUPLE OF hours later, Kelsey's phone rang, and her mother's name flashed on the screen. She picked it up and told Nash to take a break.

"Hi, Mom. What's up?"

"Is Maddy with you?" her mother all but screeched.

"No, I'm still at Nash's cabin. What's wrong?"

"I fell asleep reading. When I woke up a few minutes ago, I went to check on her and she's not in her bed. I can't find her!"

Fear grabbed Kelsey's throat. "I'll be right there. She must be hiding." She hung up and grabbed her jacket. "I'm sorry, I've got to go." Snatching up her keys, she raced out the door and slipped in the mud.

"Kelsey, what happened?" Nash asked behind her.

"Mom says she can't find Maddy. I need to get home and find her." She got in her car and tried to start it, but nothing happened when she turned the key. Her heart hammering against her chest, she opened the door and got out, started running down the slick path. It was still raining, but the air had turned much colder while she and Nash had been working.

She hadn't gotten very far when Nash pulled alongside her in his truck. "Get in!" he hollered and shoved open the passenger door.

Please be okay. Please be okay, became her mantra as they made the quick drive to her cabin.

The minute he pulled up to her door, she flung herself out and up the stairs to the front door. Lights blazed inside, and her mother rushed up to her, cradling her arm.

"I still can't find her! I'm so sorry I fell asleep."

"Mom, calm down. Let me take a look around, okay? You know she loves playing hide-and-seek. Maybe she crawled into a closet and fell asleep."

A heavy clomp sounded on the porch, and Nash limped inside. "Did you find her?"

"Not yet." She tried to keep the fear out of her voice—her mother was already near hysterical.

They methodically searched every room, closet and hiding place in the cabin.

No Maddy.

Now the panic set in, and her stomach roiled. A sob tore from her throat, and she couldn't stop the flow of tears down her cheeks.

"Shh, shh. We'll find her. I won't leave until we do," Nash said, and pulled her close to him.

She burrowed in his arms and tried to calm herself. His arms tightened around her, but his heart pounded against her chest.

"I can't lose my baby... I just can't."

"We'll find her. Now think," he said, stroking a hand down her back. "Did she say anything before you left?"

"No, she was taking..." She stepped back, had to stand on her own. "Wait, she did! She was upset because she wanted to go see the kittens. Toby and she were going to name them. I told her we'd go later. Do you think she went there by herself?"

Nash had already pulled his phone out of his pocket and pushed a button. "Dad, is Maddy up at the house?" He paused, listening, then shook his head. "We can't find her. Kelsey said she was upset earlier because she wanted to see the kittens. Yeah, I'll call Kade."

"She isn't there?"

Nash shook his head. "He hasn't seen her, and he asked

Mrs. Green, too." He dialed the phone again. "Kade, have you seen Maddy?"

Her hands itched to yank the phone from him and find out if her baby was safe and sound.

"Okay, yeah. Call the others. We'll start from this end." He shoved his phone back in his pocket. "They haven't seen her, either. Kade's calling my brothers and the ranch hands, and we're forming a search party. I'll work my way from here toward the lodge, and they'll fan out."

Her mother wailed, and Kelsey turned to see her pitch forward.

Nash got to her first, and helped her sit. "Mrs. Randolph... Bunny. Don't worry. There are a lot of people who are going to help find her." He stepped back and pulled his keys out. "Keep your phones by you, and I'll call you with updates."

Kelsey grabbed her coat. "I'm going with you. Mom, you stay here and call me if she comes home, okay?" She headed toward the front door, then stopped. "Oh! Wait a minute." Running back to the closet door, she yanked it open and searched. "Her pink rain boots and umbrella are gone."

"That'll make it easier to spot her."

The rain continued beating down, and sharp pellets stung her face. Glancing at the hood of the truck as she got in, she realized the rain was fast turning to sleet. She shut the door and clenched her hands together, trying to still the tremors. Her baby was outside in this awful weather. *It's my fault if something happens to her. We should never have come here.*

A warm hand touched hers, and she jumped. Nash's strong fingers closed around hers, and for a moment she felt safe.

"Does Maddy know how to get up to the lodge by herself?"

"I doubt it. We've always driven there." Her voice cracked, and she bit her lip, scanning one side of the road, then the other.

"She's a smart little girl. I'll bet she paid attention on the way." He squeezed her hand, and she wanted more than anything to lean on him.

But he'd said it himself—they'd be moving on before too long. Besides, she didn't want to ever have to lean on anyone again. Her heart couldn't take it.

Thomp thomp. Thomp thomp. Her heart seemed to beat in time to the wipers as they swished back and forth at a frantic pace, trying to keep the windows clear. Ice had formed on the edges not reached by the wipers.

"Does it usually get so cold in late August?"

"Not always. But it can snow any time of the year in higher elevations."

Great. One more thing to worry about.

She went back to peering out the windows, desperately searching for a bright spot of pink in the dreary gray.

Headlights flashed in front of them, and a truck pulled up beside Nash's window. She held her breath as he rolled his window down, and Kade did the same with his.

"Anything?" Kade asked.

Nash shook his head.

"Don't worry, Miss Kelsey, we'll find her!" Toby piped up from the seat next to Kade.

"Thanks, Toby," she said with a wobbly smile. She had no doubt Nash's family would do all they could to find her daughter. Tuning them out, she closed her eyes and said a silent prayer that Maddy would be found, and soon.

The movement of the truck turning around brought

her back. "What are you doing? We have to keep going, don't we?"

"My dad stationed hands along the main route to his house and the lodge. I want to go back and start from your place, try another route. Has she said anything at all about wanting to see other areas of the ranch?"

"Not really. Other than the picnic last month, we haven't ventured out much."

He sat, drumming his fingers on the steering wheel. For the first time she realized his fingers were long, strong and sturdy. Without seeing them, she knew they had calluses on them, knew how they felt against her skin. Reliable hands, hands that could take care of anything. Or anyone.

"The caves!" He suddenly gunned the gas. The truck leaped forward down the road, then he wheeled onto a side road through a thick stand of trees.

"What is it? What did you think of?" she asked, her heart about pounding out of her chest.

"When I was a little older than Maddy, I ran away from home to these caves. Stayed there so long I fell asleep. Dad was livid when they found me."

"But she's never seen them. How would she know about them?"

"She wouldn't have to. If she took this road, she'd run right into them."

The headlights cut through the darkness of the trees, illuminating the rough trail ahead of them. Tree branches scraped the sides, and she winced.

Nash parked the truck and turned the engine off. He reached in the backseat for a lockbox and put it on the seat between them. "You ever shot a gun?" he asked, pulling one out of the box.

"No, why?"

"I'm leaving this one with you. Just hold it like—"

"I'm going with you!"

"No. I don't know what kinds of wildlife could be around, and I want to concentrate on finding her, not worry about you, too."

"But—"

"I may have to crawl through some caves, and no telling if bears will already be staking them out." He pulled two cans of bear spray out of the toolbox, and her nerves shredded. "You need to be where you can watch the road in case she appears."

Why did we come to Montana, of all places? She clutched the can, but wouldn't touch the gun unless she had to.

He showed her the basics for using the gun, then laid it on the seat next to her. Opening the door, he paused, and she met his eyes. "I'll find her. I promise. I won't let anything happen to her."

"Be safe," she whispered, almost choking on her fear.

Nodding once, he shut the door. She watched him walk down the path, with only a flashlight guiding his way.

Her stomach roiled, and she swallowed several times. But it didn't help, and she barely got the door open before she tossed up everything she'd eaten that day into the bushes. Gulping big breaths of air didn't help, and she got sick again.

Climbing back into the truck, she caught a hint of Nash's scent, and it comforted her. She rooted around the backseat until she found a bottle of water and rinsed her mouth out, then stuck a wad of gum in her mouth. A litany of prayers ran through her head, over and over, as she settled down to wait for Nash's return.

You come back to me safe, Nash. And bring me my baby.

Why hadn't she told him she cared—cared as more than just his therapist? Did she even have the right to say it?

THE LIGHT SHONE steady leading the way, but shadows jumped all around him. It was eerily quiet, the wet leaves he walked on not making anything more than a squishing sound. The rocks rose in front of him, looming high. He hadn't been out here in years, since long before he left for the Army.

He shone the flashlight over the rocky hillside, scanning every crevice and dark shadow. Just as he was about to give up, he spotted the entrance to the cave about ten feet off the ground.

A branch snapped behind him, and he shifted around, flashing the light.

The trees crowded close, pressing in on him, and he tried to see through the shadows.

Something big panted to his left.

He stopped in his tracks, flashing the light toward the sound. Tried to see what was lurking in the trees, watching him.

He held still, muscles straining, ears alert for any movement.

Seconds ticked by, and he waited.

Waited to be attacked.

Waited to be ripped apart.

Waited to die.

Waited for the constant pain to end.

But now, when it mattered most, he didn't want to die.

Kelsey's face flashed through his mind—laughing, encouraging, full of life. The ecstasy on her face when she came.

Damned if I'll stand here and let her down.

Slowly backing toward the rocks, he made as much noise as he could, hoping to scare whatever it was away. His foot kicked something, and he aimed the flashlight toward it.

A pink umbrella.

Footsteps padded through the leaves. A darker shadow crossed the path just beyond the glow of light, chuffing at him.

He inhaled and smelled wet fur.

A bear.

He hoped to God her cubs were nowhere near Maddy.

He stepped back once again, and something sharp jabbed his butt. Feeling behind him, he huffed a breath of relief when he touched the rock outcropping.

The flashlight illuminated the trail up the rocks, but also outlined a rockslide. It looked fresh, and he hoped Maddy had been the one to cause it. His gut told him she was up there, and he had to get to her.

It was slow going since he could only feel his way with one good leg. Loose rocks and pebbles shifted constantly beneath his feet, slowing him even further. Anger simmered beneath despair at what he'd become, all because of a damned bomb.

"Don't think about it. Concentrate on Maddy," he muttered beneath his breath.

The path opened onto a wider ledge, and he stopped at the entrance to the cave. "Maddy?" he called softly, hoping against hope she was inside, safe. He waited, heard soft breathing.

"Maddy, honey? You in here?"

"Daddy?"

His good leg went wobbly, and he struggled to speak. "It's Nash, baby girl. I'm here to take you to your mom."

He dropped to his knees and crawled forward, flashing the light through a small tunnel.

He caught a flash of pink ahead of him, and the tunnel opened into a bigger space. "Hey, Maddy."

Maddy rubbed her eyes, and he crawled to her, dragging his left leg, his thigh burning. She flung herself forward, and he caught her, holding her close.

"You okay? Are you hurt anywhere?"

She shook her head against his shoulder and burst into tears. Sobs ricocheted off the cave walls, and her tears soaked through his already-wet shirt.

And damned if he didn't want to cry, too, he was so relieved to find her.

"Shh, it's okay, baby girl. You're safe. I'm going to take you home, okay?"

Her head moved against him, and he assumed she was nodding.

"I can't carry you. You'll have to follow behind me, okay? Can you stand up?"

"Ye-e-es," she whispered, sniffling.

He set her on her feet and turned the light back toward the tunnel. "You follow right behind me." He shuffled forward and felt her hand grab his shirt.

It was slow going, but the tunnel finally opened to fresh air heavy with ozone from the rain. Crawling out of the entrance, he stood and picked Maddy up, hugging her tight. His legs shook, and he hoped he could make it down the path.

She tightened her arms around his neck, and it was the most precious thing he'd ever experienced.

"We need to get down the hill. I know your mom is really anxious to see you. You ready?"

She nodded against him, and he set her on the ground, her little hand clutched tight in his. They started down the path. He slid on loose rocks, falling several feet down the slope before catching hold of a small birch tree.

Maddy burst into tears. "I'm s-s-s-scared!"

"It's okay," he said, pulling himself up against the hillside. "Let's try it again."

She shook her head, her curls flying.

"How about if you ride piggyback? Think that would work?"

"Okay."

He picked her up and shifted her around to his back. "Now you hold on tight." Picking his way more slowly, feeling with his good foot every step of the way, they continued down the hill.

Maddy's hands clung to his neck, her legs tight around his waist. He wanted to hurry but didn't dare for fear he'd fall with her on his back.

Ten feet had never seemed very high when he'd had two good legs. Now climbing down seemed as much out of range as the idea of him ever leading a normal life.

Now more than ever he hated his circumstances. Now when it mattered the most. Now that he had someone else's life in his hands.

They finally reached the ground, and he flashed his light around to make sure no wildlife lingered nearby. Keeping the light trained on the ground, he set a quick pace on the wet trail.

The trees thinned and the night became lighter. He headed toward the truck, and the headlights flashed on, blinding him. Stopping, he flung his arm up to shield his eyes.

"Maddy!" Kelsey cried.

He heard the truck door slam.

"My baby!"

"Mommy!" Maddy cried, and loosened her hold on him as Kelsey took her.

In the light from the truck, he saw the tears pouring down her face as she hugged Maddy tight.

She looked up at him, her lips trembling. "Thank you for saving my baby." She pulled him close and hugged him with one arm, and Maddy reached out to hug him, too.

They stood that way for long moments.

Like a family.

That shook him more than being caught in a firefight, trapped and helpless as a bomb ripped his world apart.

Chapter Fifteen

The whole way back to her cabin, Kelsey wavered between wanting to lock Maddy away for life, or to throw a party. Horrible images had flashed through her mind while she waited for Nash in the woods, and they made her sick twice more. She was ready to pack them up and move her family back to Florida, but then she'd look at Nash sitting in the driver's seat, holding Maddy's hand, and she wanted more than anything to stay.

In Montana.

With him.

You can't think that way. He doesn't want anyone in his life.

She'd grown attached to the rough, wounded cowboy, and she was heading toward dangerous territory. It would not be good to fall for him.

Unless it's too late...her heart whispered to her.

As they neared the cabin, she counted five trucks parked in front. Nash had radioed Kade, who must have spread the word they'd found Maddy. Guilt pricked her conscience at having dragged them all out on a cold, rainy day. But they'd banded together to help search for her daughter, and she'd be eternally grateful to all of them.

Nash parked and walked around to open the passenger door.

"Oh thank God! You found her!"

As soon as they reached the porch, Bunny flung her arms around Maddy. Angus had followed her outside, and gathered her mother and Maddy into his arms.

"Come on inside out of the cold. I've got hot cocoa on the stove," her mother said.

They trooped inside, and all of Nash's brothers were spread around the room, along with Toby. Angus took Maddy, wrapped her in a blanket, and sat down with her on his lap by the fire. "So you've had quite an adventure, haven't you? Where did you go?"

"I wanted to see the kitties, but I got losted on the way. Something growled at me, and I got scareded." Maddy's lower lip jutted out, and her face crumpled.

"Nash said you found a cave to hide in?"

Maddy nodded. "I remembered what Uncle Hunter told me about staying away from bears and mooses. And I saw a cave, so I climbeded and climbeded and hid."

"She was in the same cave I had run away to. Can't believe she made it all the way up there."

"Good job, son. I knew you'd step up when it counted," Angus said.

Kelsey glanced at Nash, and his face closed off. A muscle ticked in his jaw, and she knew he had to be gritting his teeth to not engage with his dad in front of everyone.

No one said a word, and it took everything within her not to jump to his defense. Somehow she didn't think he'd appreciate it.

"Nash saved me!" Maddy cried out, melodramatically. "He's my hee-wo!"

The tension broke, and they all laughed.

"But he falled down and got hurted on the rocks." She pointed to Nash, and Kelsey glanced at his left leg.

Somehow in all the excitement, she'd missed the blood on his thigh.

"Come with me. We don't want your leg to get infected. Hopefully you won't need stitches."

"But, Mommy, isn't that his fa—"

"Mother! Didn't you say something about cocoa for everyone?" Kelsey jumped in, knowing her daughter was about to spill the beans. "Angus, would you please help Mom while I tend to Nash's leg?"

Angus looked at her like she'd suddenly turned purple. "Sure thing. Come on, Bunny. I'll give you a hand." They headed out to the kitchen, hand in hand.

She grabbed Nash's arm and all but dragged him to her bedroom and shut the door. "First things first," she said, and pushed him against the door.

She kissed him, hard and fast, desperate to convey how much she appreciated him finding her daughter.

He pushed her shoulders back. "What's that for?"

"Thank you for finding my baby. You risked your life to do it, and I don't know how to thank you."

He leaned forward and kissed her lightly. "No thanks necessary. But you can keep kissing me anyway."

She stepped back and changed the subject.

"I understand you're not ready to tell your family, but they're going to have to find out one of these days. Maybe your dad would be more underst—"

"You don't get it, do you? He'll never understand. We'll never have a warm and cozy relationship, so just butt out." He turned toward the door.

"Sit down," she ground out around clenched teeth.

He glanced at her, and she jabbed a finger toward the bed, but he reached for the door handle.

"I said *sit*." And she stomped over, grabbed his arm, dragged him to the bed.

"Well, if you put it that way…" He sat on the bed and pulled her down on his lap.

"Let me up, you oaf." She pushed against him, but his arms tightened around her.

He nuzzled her throat and her traitorous body sizzled at the touch of his lips.

"Nash," she murmured. And gave up, turning her head to meet his mouth. The thick stubble on his chin tickled her jaw, and she relished the abrasion.

She traced a line of kisses along his cheek toward his ear. "Thank you for saving my baby today."

His hand slid up her stomach to cup her, and she ached for his touch.

A hoot of laughter from the living room made her jump. "We can't do this."

He stroked her cheek and stared into her eyes. She'd willingly give up everything to know what he was thinking. He'd never looked at her like this before. Could he care for her?

"What is it? Nash?"

He closed his eyes and sighed, shifting her off his lap. "Nothing." He lifted his hands up and scrubbed them across his face.

"You must be tired. Did you really fall, like Maddy said?"

He shrugged a shoulder. "I'm fine."

"I should at least check your leg. I'm worried about that blood." She slid off his lap and sat next to him. "Come on. Pull your jeans down." She expected him to turn things sexy again, but he just sighed, stood and yanked his jeans down enough for her to see his left thigh.

Rolling down the torn wrapping, she saw the scratches that abraded his skin, and the dried blood that coated his thigh. She hurried to her bathroom and got things to clean up the scrapes, then walked back to him. Sinking to the floor, she set about wiping off the blood and took care of the scratches.

"How does your prosthesis feel? Any changes?"

He shrugged. "It's fine."

"The one you were fitted for should be in soon, but I don't want you to have any problems with this one." She sat back, but noticed a gash in the denim halfway down his prosthetic, then stood up to rummage in her dresser for a sturdy needle and thread.

"I don't really need stitches, do I?"

Grinning, she thought she'd torture him a bit. "Yes. With this big ole needle."

He leaned away from her as she neared the bed again.

"Oh, don't be a baby. I thought I'd sew up the hole in your jeans for you."

Red suffused his face, and she laughed until he growled at her.

She threaded the needle and sat cross-legged on the floor.

"Don't you want me to take my pants off?"

Yes! her body cried out. "A rough stitch will do for now. I don't want to be too long in here, or they might wonder what's going on and barge in."

"Next time put a sock on the door handle," he muttered.

"You're a riot of laughs, aren't you? I don't want anyone to think poorly of me."

He shrugged again, but dang if he didn't look a little hurt.

She sewed up the rip in the denim quickly, then tied it off and bit the thread with her teeth. "All done."

He stood up and headed for the door, but paused before opening it. "Thanks for watching my back." Then he turned the handle and walked out.

She nodded, then followed him out the door into a room full of noise. Maddy sat on Hunter's lap now and seemed to be eating up the attention of all the Sullivan men.

"And next week I'll be—" she held up six little fingers "—six! And I get to be a princess!"

A chorus of deep male voices asked what day her birthday was, and they all looked to Kelsey.

"The first," she said, amazed so much time had gone by since they'd been at the ranch.

"Uh-huh, and I want a big party!"

"Maddy, no," Kelsey spoke up, embarrassed.

"Nonsense, Kelsey. We must have a party for our Madison," said Angus.

"That's too much trouble. Mom and I will have a little—"

"You forget—you and Maddy are part of our family now," he said, sliding his arm around Bunny. "Don't worry. Mrs. Green will take care of all the details. We'll invite Maddy's friends from day care."

"That's too much, Mr. Sullivan."

"I insist. And I told you before, call me Angus. Unless you want to call me Dad."

Dad?

"Thank you… Angus. But I'll help Mrs. Green with everything. She's a busy woman taking care of all you Sullivan men."

"She'll love it. Honestly. Woman loves throwing a party together, and for a little girl like Maddy, she'll be in heaven."

She looked at her daughter. "I don't know. Maddy did run away today and caused a lot of problems. Not to mention she had me and her grandmother worried sick."

Maddy's face fell.

Nash stepped forward and picked Maddy up from Hunter's lap. "I'll bet you anything Maddy is really sorry, aren't you, baby girl?"

She nodded, but her lips still wobbled.

"And I'll bet she'll be really good from now on and promise never to run off by herself again, right?"

Maddy nodded, even her curls drooping.

"What do you say, Kels? Please, can she have a party?"

Who are you, and what have you done with Nash? Has he been snatched by aliens and replaced by someone who would encourage a party?

She wavered, but caved when she looked at Maddy clasping her hands together, pleading silently. "Oh all right. But we're going to have a long talk tonight before you go to bed, young lady."

Maddy squealed, and Nash and his brothers all laughed.

On a bizarre day like she'd just had, nothing would faze her more than the image of Nash holding her daughter and convincing her to have a party.

Maybe, just maybe, there was hope for him yet.

Chapter Sixteen

A week later, Nash was in Billings, mission one accomplished: picking up the present he'd ordered for Maddy. He'd told Kelsey he had to cancel therapy, but refused to tell her why, wanting it to be a surprise. For both his ladies. The party was tomorrow, and the present had arrived just in time.

He'd just picked up the new prosthetic leg. Several times during the drive in, he'd almost wished Kelsey were there to distract him. Used to be, he'd go to Billings to pick up rodeo or ranch equipment. Now he was at a place where he had to pick up something to make him at least look normal, even if he'd never feel that way again.

He headed out the door of the medical center, carrying the box with the new leg in it to the back lot where he'd parked his truck. A crash sounded behind him, and he looked around. A man in a wheelchair, his clothes dirty and tattered, was digging through a trash can. Nash's gaze narrowed to a pinpoint focus on the man's worn camo fatigues, one pant leg flapping loose, and his breath shortened.

An amputee.

"What the hell are you staring at?" the man hollered.

Nash jerked, and he started breathing again. "Sorry," he mumbled.

"I ain't a freak show."

"Hey, look. I didn't mean to offend. You just took me by surprise."

"Ain't ever seen someone missing a body part, cowboy?" the man sneered.

Anger boiled up from within, and his heart raced. A red haze seemed to overtake his vision. "Oh yeah? I am one," he snapped, and raised his pant leg to show the hated metal leg.

"Nash?"

He looked up to see Hunter staring at his leg, his eyes wide, face gone pale.

Nash shut his eyes. *Shit!*

He cracked an eye open to see his brother standing at the edge of the lot.

Shit.

"Wha-wha—" Hunter looked up at him. "What's going on?"

Another crash sounded as the man in the wheelchair shoved the lid back on the trash can. Nash fumbled in his pocket and pulled out several bills. He walked the few steps to the man and handed it to him.

"I don't need your charity," the old guy slurred, and took a swig from a bottle wrapped in a paper bag.

"Go get yourself something to eat," Nash mumbled. He dropped the bills in the man's lap, then walked to his truck and unlocked the door, set the box inside and locked it again.

"Come on," he said, and jerked his head at Hunter. They walked a few doors down to a bar and went in. The scent of old cigarette smoke and alcohol washed over him, and he waited a beat for his eyes to adjust to the dim light. Several people were spread out along the bar, so he headed to a back booth in a secluded corner.

They slid onto the scarred wooden seats. A waitress wandered over to take their order, plunking down two bowls of peanuts.

"What the hell?" Hunter asked.

"Keep your voice down. I don't want everyone knowing."

"Everyone. You mean your *family*?" Hunter didn't bother to hide his anger.

The waitress returned and set down frosted mugs of beer and two shot glasses, then walked to the next table.

Condensation trickled down the cold glass, and Nash watched a drop trail down to the wood table.

"So?" Hunter asked.

Nash tossed the shot back, letting it burn down his throat to his roiling gut. He held up the shot glass to the bartender and gestured for two more.

"We got word of enemy troop movement and headed out to stop them from bombing a village. It was a trap. We were cornered in a canyon outside the village. If I hadn't wanted to take a shortcut, it never would have happened. We were outnumbered, and they hit us with all their firepower."

He shot back another whiskey, hoped it would dull the sounds in his head, the visions, the blood. "I watched all my men die. Then they lobbed one more IED—that's the one that got me this," he said, and slapped his left leg. He turned the beer mug around and around on the table, leaving wet rings in a concentric pattern.

His brother was silent. Nash finally looked up just as Hunter tossed back his own whiskey, then wiped his eyes.

"Shit. I don't even know what to say. Why the hell didn't you tell us? Why didn't the commander tell us when he called?"

"I made them all swear not to. I wanted to tell you in person."

"You've been home several months now. And you never said a word," Hunter said, bitterness coating his words like acid. "You don't trust us? Is that it?"

"It's my busin—"

"Don't give me that 'it's your business' crap. We're your *family*. There's no one you can trust more."

Guilt ate at Nash's stomach, and he took a long sip of beer.

"I reckon Kelsey knows, since she's your therapist. What does she think?"

He cocked a half grin. "She keeps pestering me to tell you all."

Hunter lifted his beer mug, tipped it toward Nash. "She's a smart woman. You oughta keep her, make sure she doesn't leave."

Nash lowered his eyebrows. "What are you talking about?"

"I've seen the way you look at her. She's the one for you. You need to get your head out of your ass before it's too late."

"The last thing she needs is damaged goods. She deserves better."

"Yeah, she probably does. And I don't mean because of your injury. But she's got it just as bad for you."

"She does not," he protested, even as he wondered *what if*?

"Yeah, she does. I was gonna ask her out, seeing as I'm the best-looking brother outta the bunch." Hunter smirked. "But she never looked my way. Now we're good friends."

Nash downed the last of the cold beer. "You want another?"

"Nah. I have to head over to pick up some equipment that was being repaired." He checked his watch. "I need to get outta here."

He grabbed his brother's arm before he could walk away. "You won't say anything, right?"

Hunter shook his head. "As much as I think you're being a dumbass, no, I won't." He jabbed a finger toward Nash. "But you need to, and soon, bro. And the way I see it, you didn't get your men killed. The ones you were over there fighting did it." And he walked out of the bar.

Feeling lower and grumpier than a grizzly fresh out of hibernation, he debated about having another round. But there was a three-hour trip back to the ranch ahead of him, and he really needed to be there for Maddy's birthday.

He headed out of the bar into the dim light of evening. As he got in his truck, he picked the bag containing bows up off the floor and set it gently on the seat so they wouldn't get dirty on the drive home.

When he realized what he'd done, he stopped, hand outstretched.

Only a dad would have plotted and planned and agonized over what to get his daughter.

Only a dad would buy this kind of gift for his daughter.

Only a dad would go out of his way to buy matching pink-and-white ribbons and bows for his daughter.

Maddy wasn't his daughter.

So why did he feel so protective of her? Want to put a happy smile on her face, see it light up when she saw his gift?

Chapter Seventeen

Maddy's party at the lodge was a rousing success. Kelsey would be eternally grateful to Angus for giving her daughter something she'd always remember. Most of her friends from day care came, and Angus had made sure to have entertainment for the parents, as well.

The decibel level rivaled that of a rock concert. Hamburgers and hot dogs grilled outside for the kids, and steaks for the adults permeated the air.

Maddy was in fairy princess heaven, being the center of attention of the Sullivan men—all except for Nash. He'd put in an appearance, then disappeared shortly afterward. As soon as the party was over and Maddy was settled down, she'd go check on him.

Her daughter ran past yet again, a pink cupcake in each hand. With all that sugar, the settling down part might take a while.

Hunter headed her way, his plate loaded down with steak, mashed potatoes and corn. "Hey, Kelsey," he said, sitting beside her at the picnic table decorated with a pink-and-white tablecloth and balloons.

She eyed his plate and swallowed hard, hand on her stomach, fighting the urge to be sick. "How can you eat so much and not explode? Or gain any weight? It's not fair."

He grinned around the ear of corn he was gnawing on. "How do you think?" He winked at her.

"Honestly. You men."

"Did you eat?" he asked, then shoved a forkful of potatoes in his mouth.

"Not hungry. Nerves, I guess." Picking up the glass of ginger ale, she sipped slowly hoping she'd make it out of there without puking.

She started to get up, but he stopped her.

"I know about Nash's leg."

She plopped back down on the bench, hard. The air whooshed out of her. "What do…?" Her voice squeaked, and she cleared her throat. "What do you mean?"

"I ran into him in Billings yesterday, caught him arguing with a homeless man. We had a long talk, and he told me what happened. It just gutted me he's been going through this alone."

She looked down and brushed crumbs off the tablecloth. What could she say? That it broke her heart, and she wanted to give him peace of mind, body and soul?

He toasted her, then took a swig from the bottle of soda. "I'm just real glad he's had you in his corner. Because you are, aren't you?"

Glancing up, she frowned. "Of course I'm in his corner. It's my job."

"I think it goes deeper than that."

Her mouth opened, but no protest came out.

"That's what I thought," he said, and grinned.

"Oh all right. I do care about him. But the feeling is definitely not mutual."

"That's where you're wrong. I think he's got feelings, he's just too pigheaded to act on them."

Oh, we've acted on something. Twice. Her body

flushed just thinking about being with Nash. In fact, her body seemed to crave him.

"Well, nothing will come of it." She finished the words with a huge yawn. Honestly, why was she so tired?

He looked at her, fork held midway to his mouth. "You okay? You're kind of pale."

"Just tired."

"Are you coming down with something? You haven't eaten. You're pale and tired. Maybe you should see the doctor."

She started to shake her head and suddenly realized the last time she'd felt this way, she'd been preg—

No. She'd made sure to be careful with Nash.

A loud metallic ringing sounded from the front porch.

Angus stood there with her mother by his side, ringing an old-fashioned triangle. "Folks, since we've got most of our family, friends and employees here, I wanted to let you all in on some big news. Before too long, we'll be hosting a movie crew here. They've rented out all our rooms and cabins, and will be filming here on our property."

"I can't believe he sold out," Hunter said, clunking the bottle of soda on the table.

"Sold out?"

"Dad swore he'd never have a movie crew here after the fiasco that happened at a neighboring guest ranch."

"What happened?"

"You name it—they did it or destroyed it. I need to go talk to Kade." He picked up his plate and stalked off toward his older brother.

As she listened to Angus answer questions, the late-afternoon sun started waning, and a chill drifted across her neck. Guests started leaving, and she stood to help clean up the party.

Mrs. Green walked up and took the stack of paper plates from her. "You don't need to do that, Miss Kelsey. I think someone is about to fall over from all the excitement," she said, gesturing toward Maddy sitting on a bench, her head on the table. Even her crown looked wilted.

"I guess even fairy princesses need a nap, don't they?" Kelsey kissed Mrs. Green's cheek. "Thank you for making the party so special. I'm embarrassed you all went to so much trouble for her."

"Nonsense, dear. Maddy will be Mr. Angus's granddaughter before long. I think he's hankering for all his boys to settle down, give him more grandchildren."

She thanked the older woman again, then gathered up Maddy and her wagonful of presents—presents that she had protested before the party.

Maddy fell asleep as soon as she was settled in her car seat. Kelsey drove the short distance to her cabin, trying to quell her racing thoughts. Actually, if she dug deep down, she was hurt Nash hadn't stayed at the party very long.

They reached the cabin, and she was shocked to see Nash's truck parked in front. She got out and herded a sleepy Maddy out of the car and to the porch. Just as they stepped up to the door, it opened, and he stood framed in the doorway.

"What are you doing here? Are you okay? Are you in pain?"

He grinned and shook his head, then looked down at Maddy. "I had to get some little girl's birthday present all set up."

Maddy squealed and threw her arms around his leg, then raced inside.

"You didn't need to buy her a present."

He shrugged. "I wanted to."

Curious now herself, she walked in and set her purse down just as Maddy squealed again, and louder this time.

Nash gestured to Maddy's bedroom, and she headed that way.

It was like walking into a fairyland.

White starry lights were strung around the room, woven into the drapes, along the bedposts and among her stuffed toys and dolls. A child-size table and chairs graced the corner, with brand-new stuffed animals seated in the chairs, all sporting pink-and-white bows. An elegant tea set sat on the table, with cups and saucers, plates of cookies and a beautiful teapot.

Kelsey's eyes filled as she watched Maddy examine everything, a look of wonder on her face, her eyes so bright they rivaled the tiny white star lights.

"Thank you, thank you, thank you!" Maddy cried, and flung herself at Nash's legs. "This is the bestest birthday ever!"

He patted her back, looking extremely awkward. "You're welcome. Why don't you go try it out? There's a special seat just for the fairy princess." He pointed to the one open seat... Actually, it looked more like a throne.

Kelsey stepped back out of the room and tugged on his arm till he followed her out, then pulled Maddy's door shut. She led him into the main room. "Thank you for making my baby's day so special."

He shook his head. "I didn't do anything. My dad had a party for her, and everything."

"Yes, you did. And that's just it. *You* did all this for my daughter. *You* thought of something so incredibly special. *You* went and bought her amazing gifts. *You* strung all those lights. *You* came over and set all this up, so it would be ready when we got home."

"It's nothing."

She shook her head and slid her arms around his neck. "It's not nothing. Thank you," she said, and kissed him. She poured all the love she had for this hard man into her kiss, for this man who had a heart made of marshmallow. Because who else would go to all this trouble for a little girl he barely knew?

She felt his arms slide around her, and he pressed her closer to his body. Her nipples tightened, almost to the point of pain, and she rubbed against his chest. Wished he would touch her...

Then miracle of miracles, he cupped her butt and pulled her hard against his erection. Tingles and sparks danced in her blood, and she wanted to pull him down to the floor and take him inside her.

But Maddy was just a few feet away behind a wooden door, and they couldn't do anything. She eased back a bit, until almost all that touched were their lips. His incredibly talented lips and tongue that gave her so much pleasure.

"Are you gonna marry my mommy?"

Kelsey jumped away from Nash and whirled around to face Maddy. "What did you say?"

"Are you gonna get married?" Maddy's head tilted to the side and looked like she was trying to decide whether to be happy or sad.

"Why would you think that?"

"Cuz Grandma kissed Mr. Angus, and now they're getting married."

"No, sweetie, we aren't getting married. I was just thanking Mr. Nash for getting you such a special present."

Maddy stuck her lower lip out and pouted. "Oh." She cocked her head to the other side and looked up at Nash.

"Grandma said when people kiss, it means they love each other. So you love my mommy, right?"

Kelsey bit her lip and turned her head up to look at him. His face had turned bright red, and he yanked on the collar of his shirt.

"Uh," he stuttered, then cleared his throat. "Your mom is a real special lady." He glanced at the wall behind her head. "I didn't know it was so late. I need to go and get some work done."

Fighting laughter the whole way, she followed behind him to the front door. He yanked it open and hurried out.

"Coward," she said to him.

He glanced around at her. "You better believe it." He grinned, then limped down the stairs holding on to the railing and made a beeline to his truck.

She laughed and blew a kiss to him.

He waved and took off as fast as the lead car in a drag race.

ARE YOU GOING *to marry my mommy?* kept playing on a loop in his head. No matter how loud he turned the TV, or how much whiskey he drank, it wouldn't stop.

Since Mindy had dumped him for his best friend all those years ago, he'd decided marriage would be a long way off. Then he'd lost his damn leg, and he knew he'd never get married.

So why was he now thinking of Kelsey walking toward him down an aisle? Then seeing her grow round with their baby? Maybe a little boy with her eyes and his hair?

Did he love her? He couldn't stop thinking about her, hadn't since she'd walked in his front door and took him down with her wit and her self-defense move. They may have argued and fought over his therapy, and other things, but she'd always backed him up, always been in his corner.

And in bed… God, she was amazing. For someone who thought he'd never be with another woman, she'd made him feel almost whole, like a man again.

But was that enough for love and marriage, committing to each other for a lifetime?

Hell, they'd never even gone on a date.

His thoughts turned to Maddy, and how she'd called him Daddy in the cave. He'd be honored to have her call him that. To have her look up to him like a father.

But did he have the chops for that? How would he stand up against the memories of Kelsey's first husband? He didn't think the guy had been a saint, but she'd never said anything bad about him, either.

Maybe he could get the scoop from Bunny.

A sharp pain twinged again in his thigh, and he reached for the bottle, started to pour another tumblerful.

"No," he muttered, and set the bottle down.

If he really wanted to make something with Kelsey, then he had to turn over a new leaf. No more relying on whiskey to dull the pain.

He picked up his phone and saw he'd missed a text from Kelsey.

Need to cancel therapy in a.m. Sorry.

He typed in a text to her. No prob. Dinner Tuesday night? He hit Send, then set the phone on his leg.

So it would be handy.

Not that he was anxious about her answer or anything.

A few seconds later, the text chime sounded.

Why?

> He frowned. Want to spend time with u.
> The phone sounded again.

You'll see me Monday @ therapy.

Can't. Labor Day celebration. Will u & Maddy go?

Where?

Lodge. Family does all work, employees get day off to celebrate.

Like Boxing Day?

Sorta.

Can I help?

Nope. So dinner Tuesday?

Why?

> Gripping the phone, he typed again.

Want to take u on date. OK w/ u?

> He stared at the phone, willing it to chime again, with a response. The right one.
> It was like watching paint dry with a blindfold on.
> A text chimed. Finally.

Ok

"Awesome."

See u.

Then he settled back and started plotting how to keep Kelsey and her daughter in his life.

Chapter Eighteen

Labor Day dawned bright and sunny, with a slight chill in the air. Kelsey filled a thermos with steaming chamomile tea and hoped it would calm her stomach.

"Good morning, pumpkin," her mother said as she walked into the kitchen.

"Morning. Can you watch Maddy for a couple of hours? I need to run an errand."

"So early on a holiday morning?" Bunny asked, pouring a cup of tea for herself.

"Did you have plans?"

"No. But if you're going to town, can we go with you? I need to pick up a few things myself."

"No!" She winced, hearing the harsh tone. "I mean, I'd love a little time to myself. Is that okay?"

Her mother glanced at her. "Are you all right? You look a little pale."

"I'm fine. I think the party just wore me out."

"Well, you go on into town and I'll take care of Maddy." Bunny wrote a couple of things down on a pad and handed the list to her.

"Thanks, Mom. I won't be gone too long."

Gathering her things together, she hurried out to the car, anxious to get her errand over with.

The long drive into town gave her too much time to

think, so she rolled the windows down and turned the radio up as loud as she could stand, hoping to distract herself.

Finally pulling in to town, she headed straight for the drugstore and parked. The store was almost deserted, and she quickly found the aisle she was looking for. With a fast glance around to make sure she was alone, she chose the box she needed and added it to her basket.

A couple more stops to gather the items her mother needed, and she headed to the checkout counter. She set the basket on the counter, and the clerk started ringing up her items.

"Hey, Kelsey."

She froze, recognizing Wyatt's gravelly voice. Slowly she turned her head to see him looming behind her in line. "Wyatt. What are you doing here?"

"Had to pick up a couple of things for the party today. If I'd have known you needed anything, I'd have picked them up for you." He gestured to her basket.

"Oh, no worries. Had to get some girlie things for my mom."

Even as she stared at him, his eyes glanced at the items in her shopping bags, then cut back to hers.

He studied her face. "You okay?"

She nodded, so nervous she felt like she was coming out of her skin. Yanking her wallet out, she handed over the cash, then grabbed the shopping bag and held it close. "Guess I'll see you later, right?"

"Yup."

She turned around, ready to run to the car, but dying to know if he'd seen anything.

"Drive careful, Kelsey. Keep your head on straight."

He knows. She barely nodded, then hurried out the door and to her car.

All the way back to the ranch, she worried so much that he would say something to Nash or one of his other brothers it almost made her sick.

Finally reaching her cabin, she went in and found her mother and Maddy ready to go up to the lodge to help with preparations. She handed over her mother's items, then hid the shopping bag in her closet.

Her mother had explained that Angus told her about the Sullivan tradition of giving their employees the day off to really celebrate Labor Day. The family took care of all the chores, as well as fixed a big feast for any of the workers who wanted to stay on the ranch for the day.

They drove up to the lodge and headed inside. Bunny went straight to the kitchen to help with the food, but Kelsey didn't think her stomach would hold up just yet.

The front door opened, and Kade and Toby walked in.

"Maddy! Come see how much the kittens have grown!" Toby said, and took her hand, leading her to the back of the lodge.

"Morning, Kade."

"Kelsey."

Unless it was her imagination, Kade didn't look real happy about seeing her. She had no idea what she'd done to him, but he'd been somewhat curt to her lately. There were times he looked at her as if she had a big scarlet *A* on her chest.

Or maybe that was just guilt talking, knowing what she had tucked away in her closet.

The scent of something roasting drifted out of the kitchen, and her stomach roiled. Fresh air might help, so she hurried out the door, away from the food smells, away from Kade's penetrating gaze.

Following the path led her to the corral, and she saw the big black horse that had pinned Nash galloping across it. His coat gleamed in the sunlight, his mane and tail streaming behind him as he ran.

Her breath caught at the beauty in motion in front of her. Tears pricked behind her eyelids. She wanted to be as free as that horse, galloping out of pure joy across the fields. Swallowing hard against the sob rising in her throat, she fought not to cry even as a tear trickled down her cheek.

Freedom.

Freedom from bills.

Freedom from the constant worry of making ends meet.

Freedom from worrying about what she knew deep in her heart was true.

"Hey, babe."

Nash walked up next to her and hung his arms over the top rail of the corral.

She brushed the tear from her cheek and pasted a smile on her face, but didn't turn her head.

"What's wrong?" he asked, gripping her shoulders to turn her to face him.

This time she did smile. He sounded so worried. About her.

"Nothing."

"Nothing doesn't make you cry." He brushed her cheek, catching another tear on his finger.

"I guess I just got caught up watching Midnight. He's a beautiful horse."

"Talk to me, babe. Tell me what's bothering you."

She cupped his hand to her cheek. "Honestly, it's nothing. So what can I do to help for the party?"

His eyes searched hers.

She could get lost in his blue-gray eyes. They didn't look so haunted any longer, and she was glad for him.

He'd lived through a nightmare in the war, and brought one home with him, a daily reminder of what he'd suffered and lost.

Her job was to help him live with his new leg, but she cared so deeply for him, she wanted to heal his soul. She could only do so much with therapy. She'd just have to love him, be there for him, for as long as he would let her.

If only he'd love her back.

SOMETHING WAS BOTHERING Kelsey, and Nash wished he knew what it was so he could help her. She'd been crying when he came upon her at the corral, but wouldn't tell him what had upset her.

They'd been interrupted before he could delve further, and he'd been called up to the lodge to set up for the picnic.

Every minute he'd been forced to be apart from her made him that much more anxious to be with her. Which surprised the hell out of him. When had he become so dependent on a woman?

He'd watched her throughout the afternoon. Something was still bothering her, and he could tell she was trying to cover it up.

When he was finally free to join her after the food had been cleared up, night had fallen and the big campfire pit had been fired up. The ranch employees always enjoyed this turnabout day, so they liked to linger late over the fire.

He wandered over to Kelsey and sat next to her. She looked up and smiled at him, and his breath caught. She was so beautiful, inside and out. A natural-born caregiver, she rarely took time off to enjoy herself. Flames from the fire flickered, sending shadows over her already-pale face. He couldn't help running a finger down her silky cheek.

Leaning closer, he whispered in her ear. "Having fun?"

She shivered, and nodded. "Looks like everyone has had a great time today. Pretty nice of you and your family to do this for them."

He shrugged. "Tradition."

She opened her mouth to say something, but Hunter walked up to the fire and held a guitar out to Wyatt.

Wyatt shook his head, but everyone started clapping and chanting his name. Reluctantly, he took the guitar and set it on his knee.

"Wyatt plays the guitar?" Kelsey leaned closer to him and whispered.

Nash nodded. "Just wait."

Wyatt started strumming the guitar, then began singing.

Next to him, Kelsey sat up straight and looked at Nash, her eyebrows raised. "Wow! He has a great voice."

Nash agreed, proud of his brother. For having such a great singing voice, he really hated playing in front of people and rarely made an exception.

The song continued, a haunting melody of love and loss. Nash knew his brother had been through some hard times in the years away from the ranch, and his songs always spoke to something in those years.

As Wyatt sang, at one point he opened his eyes and looked directly at him and Kelsey. He stared, then seemed to nod. Or maybe Nash had imagined it.

Kelsey shivered again, and he took off his jacket, wrapped it around her shoulders. She felt so good next to him, so he left his arm draped around her. As she leaned closer to him, he realized how right she felt next to him. Both her and Maddy.

Wyatt finished his song, and everyone clapped, then began moving to leave.

Kelsey stood. "I need to get Maddy home. She's been watching movies with some of the other kids."

"I'll walk with you." They began walking up the path lit by torches, and he put his arm around her shoulder again. But as they passed two of the outbuildings, he pulled her off the path and into the shadows.

"What—?"

He cut off her words with a kiss. It had been torture sitting next to her and not being able to kiss her all evening. She belonged in his arms, in his bed and in his life.

Slanting her head, she brought her arms up around his neck, and he pulled her closer.

This wasn't a kiss to seduce. It was a kiss to let her know how he felt, even when he couldn't form the words, or allow them out of his head. Or his heart.

He eased back, then led her once more to the path. Sliding his hand down, he twined his fingers with hers as they continued up to the lodge to gather Maddy.

Maddy was sleeping in front of the TV, and he stopped Kelsey before she could reach her daughter. "I'll get her," he whispered.

Kelsey stepped back, nodding her thanks.

He bent over and picked Maddy up, nestling her close. She tucked her head against his shoulder, and he knew this was right. He wanted to make a family with Kelsey and Maddy.

Now, he just had to convince Kelsey.

Chapter Nineteen

Nash walked up to the door of Kelsey's cabin a few minutes to seven, excitement and nerves warring with each other. Voices from inside drifted out the partially open window.

"Mom, it turned blue."

"Oh, honey. Are we happy?" Bunny asked.

"I don't know."

"Well, now you can marry Nash and stay here. Problem solved."

"No, Mom. Look what happened last time. Besides, I don't know how he'll feel about this."

"Well, you need to tell him, and the sooner the better."

"I know. But maybe I should make an appointment first, just to make sure. These things aren't always accurate."

"That would be wise."

"I wonder if there are any obstetricians in town."

"Just know that whatever you decide, I'm here for you, sweetie."

Obstetrician?

Nash's heart dropped so fast he thought he'd pass out. His head whirled, thoughts spinning, and he couldn't grab one long enough to focus. He didn't want her to think he'd been eavesdropping, so he walked back to the truck and opened the door, then slammed it loud enough the metal clanged.

He headed back to the front door as it opened, and Kelsey stood framed in the doorway.

His heart just about stopped dead to see her wearing a long, flowery skirt, topped with a white blouse, and a denim shirt, tied at the waist. And cowboy boots.

He stared at her, not sure what to say, trying to interpret how she was feeling.

"Hi," she said.

"Hi." He cleared his throat. "You look beautiful."

"I wasn't sure what to wear."

"You look great. Ready to go?" He hoped so, because he didn't want any conversation with Bunny.

She nodded, and he opened her door, helped her in, stood stock-still just breathing in her scent.

Shaking his head, he berated himself as he went around the hood and climbed in. He waved at Bunny and Maddy as they stood in the doorway, then pulled out onto the road.

Just after he passed beneath the ranch sign, he pulled the truck to the side of the road.

"Did you forget something?" she asked.

He nodded. "Yeah. I forgot this." He cupped her face in his hands and kissed her, long and sweet, letting his lips just slide over hers, drinking her in. He pulled back and looked at her face. Her eyes were still closed, her mouth partially open.

"You okay?"

Her eyes opened, and she nodded.

He wondered what was going through her head, and if she would decide to tell him she might be pregnant.

A COUPLE HOURS later, they were back on the road to the ranch. He was about to come out of his skin because she hadn't said anything. She'd been distant, withdrawn, and just picked at her food, claiming to be tired. He'd tried to fill the conversational lags with stories about the rodeos he'd been in and anecdotes about growing up with his brothers.

As they neared the ranch, he turned on the side road that led to his favorite spot at the pond.

"Where are we going?" she asked.

He parked and turned off the engine. "Want to kiss you, but didn't think you'd want to do it right in front of your cabin."

Silence descended fast, the only sound the pings as the engine cooled down.

He unhooked his seat belt, then hers, and slid closer to her, brushed her hair back over her shoulder. Leaning close, he whispered in her ear, "Unless you don't want to get kissed in the moonlight."

It was dark in the truck so he couldn't see her expression, but the shiver trembling through her body encouraged him.

Lifting his hand, he slid a finger along her jawline, turned her head to face him. Moving slow, he kissed her, coaxing her lips open. When her tongue met his, he groaned, his body instantly going hard.

Her fingers gripped his shirt, her nails lightly scoring his chest. "Nash," she whispered his name, over and over, until she moved in closer to him, her fingers running feather-soft through his hair.

He cupped her breast and squeezed lightly. She gasped, and he felt her fingers slide over his, pressing his hand tighter to her.

"I want you, Kelsey," he groaned. "So damn bad." He

ran a hand down her leg, then slid her skirt up until he felt the smooth skin of her thigh.

He was too old to be necking, or anything more, in the front seat of his truck, but damn if he wasn't about to explode.

She stilled his hand on her leg. "I don't have anything with me. We need to stop."

"It's not like you can get pregnant again, right?"

The minute he said the words, he wanted to yank them back.

"Excuse me?" she asked, her voice stone cold.

He saw the shadow of her arm lift up, and the overhead light came on, blinding him. Once he could see again, he noticed her eyes had slitted, and her lips were pressed together.

"You want to repeat that?" she said, her arms crossing over her chest.

"I'm sorry. I shouldn't have said it that way. I got to your cabin a little early, and I heard you and your mom talking through the open window."

She didn't say anything, but he heard a sniffle from her side of the truck.

"Shouldn't we at least talk about this?"

"Nothing to talk about."

"You're going to the doctor to make sure, right?"

She nodded.

"Want me to go with you?" *Why the hell did I say that? I'd rather get my wisdom teeth put back in, let them get impacted, then have them pulled back out again.*

Taking a deep breath, he searched for patience and started the engine, then backed out the way he'd come. "If you are, then don't worry. I'll do the right thing and stand by you. Okay?"

Silence reigned, and the atmosphere in the Ranger was

as cold as a deep Montana blizzard. He couldn't interpret the one-and-only glance she'd thrown at him. She looked hurt, but he couldn't figure out why, since he'd offered to be there for her.

The short drive to her cabin felt like twenty miles, and he was relieved to pull up to the driveway.

"If you don't want me to go—" *slam* "—with you, at least tell me what he says." The last of his sentence was said to the wind she was gone so fast.

He finally began to understand why someone had written a book about men and women being from two different planets.

And why he felt as if he were on planet Hell.

Chapter Twenty

It was official.

A baby.

Back in the same boat as before.

Only last time she'd been confident Rob loved her, had wanted to marry her and start a family.

The miles back to the ranch ticked off slow as an iceberg moving across the sea.

She thought back to two nights ago, when Nash had said he'd *do the right thing* and *stand by her*.

Not one word about becoming a family.

Not one word about being happy.

Not one word about loving her.

That's the one that hurt the most, considering she'd gone and fallen in love with the idiot.

She'd been blindsided when he mentioned the pregnancy and hadn't known what to say.

When his only words were about responsibility and nothing about his feelings, it felt as if she'd been stabbed. Granted, her hormones were all over the place, but she hadn't expected him to talk of being together like it was a duty.

He may have thought she was being bitchy, but the truth was, the pain cut so deep she didn't trust herself to say anything without melting into a crying mess of hurt feelings and pregnancy hormones.

Now, with the pregnancy confirmed, she'd give him one more chance. Turning onto the ranch property, she headed toward his cabin, but on the way, saw his truck parked by the barn.

"Might as well get it over with," she muttered to herself, pulling up her proverbial big girl maternity panties when all she wanted to do was keep driving as far as her piece of shit car would take her, then lick her wounds.

She parked and climbed out of her car, heading toward the barn. A muffled curse made her pause, then she continued on, forcing one foot in front of the other. Peering inside the cavernous space, she saw Nash at the opposite end, outside his horse's stall. He was bending over, holding Thunder's hoof and using some tool on it.

"Is Thunder hurt?" she asked, trying to keep the tremble out of her voice.

Nash looked up, then gently set the horse's hoof down. "Just a rock." He smoothed a hand down the horse's flank, then led him into the stall.

Trying for a peace offering, she got a scoop of oats and put them in Thunder's feed bucket.

"Thanks," Nash said, coming out and closing the stall door.

"So," she said, and took a deep breath. "I'm sorry for the way I behaved the other night. I was pretty much in shock."

He moved closer to her, and she looked up at his face, aching for him to understand, to take her into his arms. Tell her it would be okay.

"I figured that much out later on." He picked up a strand of her hair and twirled it around his finger. "Find out anything?"

She nodded.

"And?" he asked, a slight croak in his voice.

She nodded again.

"Okay," he said, and blew a breath out. "So here's the plan."

"Oh, you have a plan, do you? Well don't keep me in suspense."

"We can get married right away, if you want. I'll pay for everything, and since your cabin is bigger, I can move in there with you and Maddy. That way I'll be on hand to help with anything you need."

Fighting for a calm tone, she squared her shoulders. "Is that it? All of your plan?"

He frowned. "Yes. Well, wait, there is one more thing."

One more thing, like you love me? she hoped.

"If at some point after the baby is born, you were to meet someone and fall in love, I'll let you go. But I insist on being part of the baby's life. It's half-mine, after all."

Her blood turned to ice water, and she really fought hard not to punch his lights out. She stalked away from him.

"You'll let me go if I fall in love with another man. Just like that, you'll unbuckle my leash and let me go." Her voice shook, and an intense heat flooded her body. Sweat broke out on her forehead, and she swiped it away.

"I'd understand. If you find someone, a whole man, to love, I'd understand. I want you to be happy."

"A whole man?" Grabbing a currycomb off the bench, she planted her feet wide, and threw the comb at him. It bounced off his chest and fell to the floor.

His eyebrows raised high. "Hey, calm down. It's okay." He walked forward and reached for her shoulders, but she jerked away.

"Goddammit, you are a whole man! You lost a leg, not your life, you stupid, pigheaded dumbass!"

Rage kept bubbling up from within, followed by the most acute hurt and betrayal. She clawed at her chest, trying to breathe. This hurt worse than the moment she'd found out Rob had died.

"I'm so in love with you, and this baby would have loved you, you big jerk!" She turned around and kicked a bucket out of her way, sent it skittering across the floor, oats flying along the way. "You'll let me go if I fall in love with someone else," she muttered, looking for something else to kick or throw at him.

"Kelsey—" He grabbed her arm.

With every ounce of her being, she shoved him backward, and he fell on a pile of hay.

"Don't. Don't touch me. Ever again. I'm done."

She turned on her heel and almost ran into Angus, who stood there with his mouth hanging open. "Thanks for hiring me, and for the use of your cabin." She jabbed a finger at his chest. "And you better take good care of my mother, or I'll come back here and kick *your* ass."

The door slammed behind Kelsey and echoed across the rafters of the barn. Nash's world was caving in all around him. He lay on the pile of hay, her words screaming through his head.

A pair of legs crowded into his vision, and he looked up to see his dad. "Get up, son."

He tried to scramble up, but didn't have his left foot placed right, and he fell back. His dad reached a hand out, and Nash latched on, let his dad pull him up.

He absently brushed bits of hay off his jeans, avoiding eye contact with his father.

"So, you lost a leg, huh?"

Nash nodded.

"I guess that makes sense," his dad said, his voice catching. He reached toward Nash, and he was shocked when his dad hugged him tight. "I love you no matter what, Nash. Always."

Nash stepped back, and his dad cleared his throat. "I know I haven't always been a good father, and I tend to push too hard. But I love all my boys, and I want you to be happy."

"Yeah, you did push hard. Pushed me at sports, pushed me on the ranch. Eventually, it pushed me away."

His dad closed his eyes, took a deep breath. "You're right. I had to be mom and dad to you boys, and it was the hardest thing I've had to do, besides laying your mother to rest. I guess I buried my feelings the day her coffin went in the ground."

"We've never really talked about it."

"I know. I felt as if I'd died along with her, but I had to continue on for you boys. Keep a roof over our heads, build up the ranch."

"The ranch." Nash snorted. "It always felt as if the ranch was your firstborn instead of me, and you gave *it* all your attention and love." The words just kept bubbling up, along with the pain of childhood.

"I made a lot of mistakes, but I promised your mother I'd continue on with our plans to build the ranch up into what it is now. A place she'd be proud of. I'm sorry, son."

A surprising warmth flooded Nash. "We've always butted heads. I had to leave when I did. I felt suffocated by you, the ranch. I had to find my own way." He rubbed the back of his neck. "Didn't turn out the way I expected, but it brought me back here. Thanks for letting me come home, Dad."

"It'll always be your home. For all of you."

Nash realized this was the longest conversation they'd had in years. Maybe ever. It felt good to get it all out. Except now *he'd* been the one to push the love of his life away.

"So," his dad said, clearing his throat. "A baby, huh?"

Nash nodded.

"You love her?"

Nash nodded.

"Did you tell her?"

He thought back through their conversations— disasters, really—and slowly shook his head. She loved him, and he'd driven her out by being afraid to express his own feelings.

"Sounds like you need to go over there and tell her, then get her to the altar before I get her mother there."

Nash nodded, like a brokenhearted bobblehead.

"So get moving!" his dad said, and clapped him on the shoulder.

He started to leave the barn, but turned back. "Do you still have Mom's ring?"

His dad grinned. "I do. You want it?"

"Yeah. I want to do this right."

They left the barn and walked up the path to his dad's house. "I've got it in the safe in the den."

While he waited, Nash looked at the pictures on the mantel of his parent's wedding day. They'd looked so happy. He hoped he hadn't screwed it up with Kelsey. The realization that he loved her shook him to his toes, and he was desperate to get to her, make things right.

"Here it is," his dad said, and handed him a ring box.

"Thanks, Dad."

"Your mom would be happy to know you're going to give it to someone you love. All she wanted was for each of you to be happy."

Nash nodded and started to leave, but stopped and looked back at his dad. "You know, I think she'd be happy to know you've found someone to love after all this time," he said, his voice gruff.

"Thanks, son." He cleared his throat. "Now go get your girl."

Just as he opened the front door, a truck pulled in and Bunny hopped out, crying. She saw him, and headed his way. "What did you do to my daughter?"

"It's a misunderstanding. I'm heading over to your cabin now," he said, and pulled his keys out of his pocket.

"You're too late. She's gone, and it's all your fault," Bunny cried, and raised a handkerchief to her eyes.

His dad had followed him and took Bunny into his arms.

"What do you mean? She left? That fast?" Fear clutched at his stomach, and acid burned up his throat.

"Yes. She rushed inside, grabbed a few things for her and Maddy, then took my granddaughter and hightailed it off the ranch."

"Where's she going?"

"I don't know. She said she would find a place and send for her things. She's out there all alone, with a little girl and a baby on the way, and you didn't stop her."

He started to leave, but she clutched his arm. "You need to understand something. When she and Rob were dating, she got pregnant. They got married right away, but they had some rocky times. She's scared, Nash. Back then, she knew they were going to get married, and they loved each other. When he died, I didn't think she'd ever fall in love again. But she did. With you."

His throat tightened, and he fought to inhale. He'd

screwed this up on so many levels, when all he'd wanted was to give her a way out if she didn't love him.

"What are you going to do about this?" his dad asked.

"Whatever it takes."

Chapter Twenty-One

A month later, Maddy walked slowly in front of her, dropping rose petals and wearing a miniature blue dress that matched her own. Kelsey walked down the aisle next as matron of honor for her mother. She kept her eyes on the minister and refused to look at any of the men lined up next to Angus.

Because that's where Nash would be standing. And it still hurt too much to see him. She and Maddy had settled down in Boise for the time being, and she'd gotten a therapy job with the big hospital in town. It'd been the hardest thing in her life to stay away from him, but she'd gotten through it, one lonely damn day at a time.

Her mother told her he'd been devastated when she left, but if he was willing to let her go if she fell in love with someone else, then any feelings he had for her couldn't have been too deep.

But she'd had to go back to the ranch for her mother's wedding, wouldn't let her down by not showing up. So she'd sneaked into the lodge, where her mother was getting ready, and now it was time for the ceremony. Her mother hadn't been too happy that they wouldn't be staying for the whole reception, but understood it was too hard for her to be so close to Nash.

The minister droned on, and she kept her eyes on her

mother. Only once did she slip and look at Nash. She agreed with her mother's description—he did look haggard. Dark circles smudged the skin beneath his eyes, and he hadn't shaved in quite a while. Even his cheekbones looked gaunt, and lines of pain bracketed his mouth.

The therapist in her wanted to help him get better, to stop the pain. The woman in her just wanted to love him and take care of him. And dammit, she did still love him. He turned his head to stare at her. She averted her eyes and swore not to look at him again.

Her mother handed her the bouquet of white roses and put her hands in Angus's as they repeated their vows.

A couple more hours, and she and Maddy would be leaving again, this time for much longer. A lump rose in her throat as the minister pronounced Bunny and Angus husband and wife.

THE RECEPTION WAS in full swing at the lodge, and Kelsey's nerves were so shredded she was about to scream. Every time she turned around, there was Nash, staring at her, looking so freaking handsome in his tux.

She'd stuck it out as long as she could, and now she had to escape. Spotting Maddy playing with Toby, she headed her way.

"Maddy, honey, we need to go now."

"I don't want to."

"Sweetie, we have a long drive to get home."

"This is our home," Maddy said, pouting.

"Not anymore. Come on, honey. Let's go say goodbye to Grandma."

Maddy's face crumpled, and she sniffed.

Oh please. No tears! I'm barely keeping it together myself.

She hurried through their goodbyes to her mom and

Angus, wished them well, then headed out to her car. Thank goodness she'd had the foresight to put the tote bags with their regular clothes in the car earlier. They could change at a rest stop.

"Kelsey, wait."

She looked behind her and saw Nash heading toward her. Her stomach clenched, and nerves warred with butterflies. Last thing she wanted was a confrontation with him now. She quickened her pace, but Maddy dragged her feet. Bending over, she picked her daughter up and raced to the parking lot.

Finally she and Maddy reached her car, and she jammed the key in the lock. She popped the locks and opened the back door, got Maddy settled, then climbed in. She hit the lock button, and it sounded like a death knell.

Her hands shook so bad, she could barely get the key in the ignition.

Nash knocked on her window. "Open the window."

She shook her head.

"God, babe, I just want to talk to you."

She turned the key, but the car just groaned. *Seriously?* She tried again, but nothing more than a grating groan ripped through the air.

"If you won't talk to me, at least pop the hood and let me look at the problem," Nash called through her window.

She cranked her head to the side and looked for the doohickey to pop the hood. It gave, and he walked around the front of the car, opening the hood up all the way.

With the hood blocking her view, she couldn't tell what he was looking at, but no way would she get out. Something flew past her side window, and she peeked out to see what it was.

A white wire lay on the ground. Seconds later, another

wire joined it, then suddenly wires and car parts were raining down on the ground. Completely at a loss as to how he was fixing the engine, she popped the locks and opened her door, then climbed out.

"What are you doing? How is that fixing my car?"

"Not fixing it," came his voice from the front of the car.

"What do you mean you're not fixing it?" She rounded the hood and her mouth fell open. He held a bunch of wires and stuff she had no idea the names of any of it. "You need to put all that stuff back in right now, Nash. I mean it! I can't afford a mechanic," she said, hating that her voice quavered.

He dropped the wires and reached for her hands, but she pulled free and turned away.

His hand gripped her arm, and he tugged her back around. "Come home with me, Kelsey."

"Why, so you can *set me free* when I meet someone else?"

His eyes closed, and he grimaced. "I deserve that. I made a complete mess of it trying to do the right thing."

"Yeah, you did."

"I'm sorry. You have no idea how sorry I am. I about pestered your mom to death to find out where you went. She wouldn't break." He pulled her close, and she breathed him in, wanted to relax against his solid warmth. But she had to be strong. Had to get back to her new life.

Without him.

"Can you ever forgive me?"

Shoving hard, she stepped back. "You can't give me the one thing I want, Nash."

He opened his mouth, his brow furrowing.

"And if you have to ask what it is, you'll never understand." She jerked away from him and turned to head back inside to find someone to help her, but froze. There were at least fifty people, if not more, watching them. The Sullivan family and her mother were in the very front.

"I love you."

She whirled around. "What?"

"I love you, Kelsey. I think I fell for you the minute you walked into my cabin and stood up to me and my brothers. I loved you when you kept pushing me to work harder so I could get better. I loved you when you yelled at me and pushed me into that pile of hay."

He fumbled in his pocket and pulled out a small box. He hiked up his pant leg and took a step forward, then knelt down.

A collective gasp rose from the people watching, and she looked down to see his prosthesis glinting in the late-afternoon sun.

"Nash," she hissed. "Your leg is showing."

"I don't care. It's a part of me. My family knows now, I've been going to a counselor, working through the PTSD issues. I've learned to live with it, to let go of the guilt. I just want you back in my life. I need you, babe. You and Maddy, and this little guy or girl—" he put his big, strong hand on her baby bump "—are my entire world. I love you, all three of you."

He opened the box and pulled a beautiful diamond ring from it. "This was my mom's ring. It came to me when she died. If you don't like it, we can find something else."

She sniffled and grabbed the handkerchief out of his jacket pocket, then wiped her eyes.

"I'm sorry for being such an ass. When I heard you thought you were pregnant, I freaked out."

She snorted through her tears. "You can say that again."

"I didn't want you to feel pressured into marrying me just for the baby. I didn't know how you felt about me, so instead I blundered and said the wrong things." He cleared his throat. "So now I'm saying all the right things, I hope." He glanced out at the people watching them, and a hint of red spread across his cheeks.

"Kelsey Anne Summers, will you marry me, and let me adopt Maddy as my daughter, and give me the chance to be the father of this baby? I promise to love you the rest of my life, and take care of our family, and do whatever it takes to make you happy."

She hesitated, searching for the truth in his eyes, until she felt a hard nudge from behind. Stumbling a little, she righted herself and laughed when Maddy nudged her toward Nash again.

"Nash Sullivan, I'm saying yes to everything you offered, and more."

He grinned and stood up, catching her in his arms. They whirled around and around until she was dizzy, and he put her back on her feet. He cupped her cheeks, and her breath caught when his eyes glistened.

"I'm so sorry I hurt you, babe. I promise to always love you."

"And what if I meet someone else—"

He kissed her, hard and fast. "Ain't gonna happen. I'll keep you so happy in and out of bed you won't even look at another man," he whispered in her ear.

She grinned. "I'm going to make you keep that promise, cowboy." She wrapped her arms around his neck and tugged his head down, then kissed him. "I love you, Nash."

Her world narrowed to the feel of his lips on hers, and she barely heard the applause from the people witnessing their spectacle.

"So I get to be a flower girl again, right, Mommy?" Maddy tugged her skirt, and everyone laughed.

Nash bent over and picked her up. "You okay with me being your daddy, baby girl?"

Maddy nodded, and flung her arms around his neck.

He pulled Kelsey close again, and the three of them stood there. Circled within his arms, pressed against him, she was home. And nothing else mattered now.

Chapter Twenty-Two

Nash pulled Kelsey tighter against his body, reveling in the feel of her. Now if only they were naked, he'd be even happier. He tried to move in time to the music, but every so often, there was a hitch in his gitalong. Three months ago, he never would have been on display like this, in front of people, even if they were family.

He knew now it had been pride more than anything that had had him keeping his secret as long as he had. He'd been so afraid to see looks of pity on the faces of those he loved that he'd shut them out. It had taken Kelsey and her love to bring him around.

They'd had a long talk about her job and his position on the family ranch, not sure if they'd stay on or not. But his own father had been the one to come up with a solution. Nash would continue on with his share of the ranch and horse training, and Kelsey would begin an equine therapy program for veterans. He'd help out when needed in her program. They'd applied for the licenses required, gotten everything in order and already had a line of soldiers wanting to sign up.

Now they were dancing at their wedding reception, and he just wanted to be alone with her. Once she'd agreed to marry him, her mom had kicked in to overdrive and put together a wedding in a week. They'd have been just as happy going in front of a judge, but Bunny Randolph-Sullivan would have none of that. And she'd done a pretty good job of throwing together a nice wedding for them, complete with a white dress and white cowboy boots for Kelsey.

"Doin' all right, Mrs. Sullivan?" he whispered in Kelsey's ear.

She trembled in his arms, and he couldn't wait to make her shiver more later that night.

"Doin' just fine, Mr. Sullivan." She grinned up at him.

"Kelsey," Bunny said, stepping up to them. "It's time to throw the bouquet so you can leave."

Kelsey stepped back and took the bouquet from her mother while the DJ told all the single women to gather at the edge of the dance floor.

He moved off to the side and saw Wyatt talking with a pretty blonde as she walked to the group. He rolled his eyes. Did he have to hit on every woman in the vicinity? Now that he was an expert on love, he wanted his brothers to settle down and be happy.

Kelsey laughed as she turned her back on the group, and held the bouquet in her hands.

"Three…two…one!" she called out, then tossed the bouquet of white roses over her head and into the crowd.

A few petals flew from the blossoms as the bouquet struck a target—Wyatt's head—and left a few white rose petals clinging to his dark hair.

Wyatt grabbed the bouquet, more out of reflex, and looked down at it, his eyebrow rising, then a look of profound fear crossed his face.

"Hey! Kelsey! You need to do that over again," Wyatt hollered, holding it out to her.

Kelsey was bent over laughing, then stood up and

wiped her eyes. "Oh no, brother-in-law, it was meant to be. One of these days, you'll be walking down the aisle!"

Nash couldn't help the laugh bubbling up from his gut, and he busted out at the expression on his brother's face. He kissed his new bride, and said to Wyatt, "I just hope you find someone who can kick your butt into line like I did, bro."

He whisked her away, as fast as he could with a less pronounced limp, to their cabin.

On the porch, he pulled her into his arms.

"Thanks for taking a chance on me, Kelsey." He kissed her cheeks, her nose, her eyelids. "You saved me from a very dark future. You brought hope and happiness back into my life. You gave me a reason to wake up every day. Most of all, you gave me love."

He kissed her until they were both breathless.

Then he gently picked her up, cradling her in his arms, and crossed the threshold into their home, and into the bright future they would make together.

* * * * *

MILLS & BOON

Coming next month

BABY SURPRISE FOR THE
SPANISH BILLIONAIRE
Jessica Gilmore

'Don't you think it's fun to be just a little spontaneous every now and then?' Leo continued, his voice still low, still mesmerising.

No, Anna's mind said firmly, but her mouth didn't get the memo. 'What do you have in mind?'

His mouth curved triumphantly and Anna's breath caught, her mind running with infinite possibilities, her pulse hammering, so loud she could hardly hear him for the rush of blood in her ears.

'Nothing too scary,' he said, his words far more reassuring than his tone. 'What do you say to a well-earned and unscheduled break?'

'We're having a break.'

'A proper break. Let's take out the *La Reina Pirata*—' his voice caressed his boat's name lovingly '—and see where we end up. An afternoon, an evening, out on the waves. What do you say?'

Anna reached for her notebook, as if it were a shield against his siren's song. 'There's too much to do . . .'

'I'm ahead of schedule.'

'We can't just head out with no destination!'

'This coastline is perfectly safe if you know what

you're doing.' He grinned wolfishly. 'I know exactly what I'm doing.'

Anna's stomach lurched even as her whole body tingled. She didn't doubt it. 'I . . .' She couldn't, she shouldn't, she had responsibilities, remember? Lists, more lists, and spreadsheets and budgets, all needing attention.

But Rosa would. Without a backwards glance. She wouldn't even bring a toothbrush.

Remember what happened last time you decided to act like Rosa, her conscience admonished her, but Anna didn't want to remember. Besides, this was different. She wasn't trying to impress anyone; she wasn't ridiculously besotted, she was just an overworked, overtired young woman who wanted to feel, to be, her age for a short while.

'Okay, then,' she said, rising to her feet, enjoying the surprise flaring in Leo di Marquez's far too dark, far too melting eyes. 'Let's go.'

Continue reading
BABY SURPRISE FOR THE
SPANISH BILLIONAIRE
Jessica Gilmore

Available next month
www.millsandboon.co.uk

LET'S TALK
Romance

For exclusive extracts, competitions
and special offers, find us online:

 facebook.com/millsandboon

 @millsandboonuk

 @millsandboon

Or get in touch on 0844 844 1351*

For all the latest titles coming soon, visit
millsandboon.co.uk/nextmonth